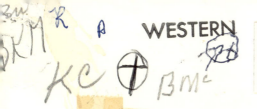

THE
BLUE BASIN
COUNTRY

By the Same Author
In Thorndike Large Print

SPIRIT MEADOW
THE PERALTA COUNTRY
THE NEW MEXICO HERITAGE
THE HORSEMAN
THE HOMESTEADERS
THE MARSHAL
SKYE
TANNER

THE
BLUE BASIN
COUNTRY

Lauran Paine

Thorndike Press • Thorndike, Maine

Library of Congress Cataloging in Publication Data:

Paine, Lauran.
    The Blue Basin country.

    Reprint. Originally published: New York
Walker, 1987.
    1. Large type books.   I. Title.
[PS3566.A34B53   1989]   813'.54   88-29654
ISBN 0-89621-241-6 (alk. paper)

Large Print edition available in North America by arrangement
with Walker and Company.

Cover design by Michael Anderson.

Contents

THE
BLUE BASIN
COUNTRY

CHAPTER 1
SPRINGTIME

The boundaries of the Blue Basin country were vaguely defined, as calculations made by eye often are. The Army Engineers who had passed through years earlier surveying and mapping had missed it entirely, which was understandable in a country where mountain ranges of awesome height and depth — along with seemingly limitless flowing oceans of land — dwarfed surveying parties to less than ant-size. The effect of such mind-numbing, thousand-mile expanses of land had been to create in the engineers a sensation of urgency, along with a feeling of futility. The entire region could not possibly be surveyed, so the conclusion was to only chart and map areas which were seemingly important.

The Blue Basin country had been insular even back then. Towns emerged slowly without planning, ordinarily as wattle-roofed low buildings with log walls. They began as points of rendezvous for trappers, hunters, soldiers. Later they expanded to accommodate the traffic of roadways used by wagons, coaches, pack-trains, horsebackmen.

Settlement of the area was not a quick process, except to those who had watched the hide and trapping trades diminish. For these people, changes quickly forced them to decide whether to move on or stay put.

Holtville, which served the Blue Basin country, was a community with such a heritage. In some ways vestiges of those rough earlier days still showed, like the massively functional log walls of several business establishments in town. In other ways the change was complete — in the middle of miles of open grassland (without even underbrush, let alone standing trees) Holtville's Main Street was lined on both sides with large, handsome sycamore trees.

Unlike a number of communities with similar beginnings, Holtville made each required transition without the wrenching adjustments that commonly troubled other towns. And because changes appeared to answer pressing needs, not even the old hide hunters and packers did much complaining. For example, since there was an overabundance of grassland no one used anyway, no one objected when cattlemen drove big herds into Blue Basin. As the cattle ranches needed Holtville as their base for supplies, inevitably the economy grew and stabilized; the arrival of the stock-men was viewed as a godsend, not as a cause for resentment or grumbling.

This was the background that ensured per-manence for the town. It was also the culmi-nating sequence of events which blurred the distinction between growth and progress among the settlers of Blue Basin. If any of them ever thought about it at all, it was proba-bly as a thing called manifest destiny, a popu-lar term at the time but whose interpretation was very different west of the Missouri River than it was in Washington, the nation's capi-tal.

In the Blue Basin country manifest destiny meant that people were *there;* the land was there; it was free, abundant, available for whatever people wanted to do with it or make of it. Therefore, with winter fading and wood-sheds low, it was the right — in fact the obli-gation — of people to head for the mountains for firewood logs with wagons stripped to their running gear.

This was less a rite of spring than it was the result of the customary autumn wood cutting being limited by the cutters' inaccurate esti-mates of how many cords would see them through the winter, with the factor for error compounded by aching backs, on the one hand, and the unpredictable weather, on the other. Springtime was supposed to arrive in late March or April. But some years there were black frost, frozen troughs, and snow flurries right on up into late May.

It was that kind of a year when Abel Morrison and two other men set out to cut some wood. Abel, the Holtville saddle and harness maker, had something called vaguely 'heart trouble.' Alexander Smith, who only had one eye and hid the adjoining empty socket behind a white patch, was owner of the Holtville Gun Works. The third man was Foster Bullard, who was irrepressible, defiantly good-natured and had a bad lower back.

They loaded Abel's old wagon bed with tools, grub, and a tent of rotten canvas with dozens of patches, put Alex Smith's two eighteen-hundred-pound draft horses on the pole, and headed northeast toward a high prairie which was surrounded by huge fir trees, sprinkled throughout with snags. They went for the snags, those standing dead trees, usually full of woodpecker holes stuffed with acorns, that popped like bullets in a stove. Snags were dry wood. If people needed wood to burn, green fir was as useless as teats on a man. It wouldn't burn, and sometimes it wouldn't even smoulder or smoke; it simply filled a stove or woodshed with something no one could use until it had dried out. Men who went up into the mountains to 'make wood' in springtime did so only for one reason: they had to have something that would burn right then, not next fall.

The three knew where the snags were. Among the big trees that ringed a high plateau inhabited by wild horses, a few wapiti, and some varmints such as brown bears and big cats. It was a daylong drive to get up there, so the old men had left town well ahead of sunrise, when it was cold as well as dark. About darkness they could do nothing; about the cold they had an excellent remedy: they were almost to the old military road leading upward before Foster fished in a croaker sack and handed around a bottle of pop skull; and ten minutes later had insulated each man against the chill.

Initially, they talked, speculating on what they would find and when they would be loaded and ready to head down. Then they covered the areas of rumor and gossip.

The year before, for example, John Holbrook — who owned thousands of acres, ran red-back cattle, kept four fulltime riders and was known to be both wealthy and short-tempered — had been operated on for an obsidian bird-arrow that had been lodged in a vertebra for over fifteen years. What intrigued the woodcutters was Holbrook's decision to have the surgery when the best doctors up in Denver had told him if it failed, he might never walk again.

The woodcutters were Holbrook's age or thereabouts; each of them knew him and, as Abel said after leaning over the side to spray amber, before the operation old John hadn't been able to straddle a horse or work at the marking grounds in years. Nor had he ever been entirely free of pain. Abel spat again, ran a heavy glove across his lips and also said, " 'Course a man can't come right out an' say what he'd do — but I think he did exactly right."

Alex, who was favoring the big horses that were all the family he had, nodded thoughtfully. "Yes, he done right. It seems to me when a man gets old enough to know something's not goin' to get better, only maybe worse, and he's already done everything at least once — when he's no good to himself or anyone else — takin' that kind of a risk don't measure up to but one choice. An' if he'd come out of it paralyzed from the middle down, well, there's worse things than suicide, isn't there?"

No one replied. The horses were leaning into their collars now going up around the slope leading to the big plateau. It was natural that each man watched the big rumps ahead.

Alex did not take his one good eye off his horses when he said, "I'm still cold. How about you fellers?"

Abel punched Foster in the ribs, otherwise Bullard would not have understood the implication. He leaned, groped in the sack again, and handed Alex the bottle.

The pop skull made another circuit and was stowed in the croaker sack as Alex said, "Old John had a good year. Got his back patched, married that pretty girl of his to that horse-breaker who's got a scrub-ranch west of the Holbrook place a few miles . . . " Alex interrupted himself to call quiet encouragement to the big horses; they had one last hard pull up over the lip of the slope to the big meadow.

Nothing more was said until they were up there, then Foster Bullard screwed up his face. "I can't remember that horsebreaker's name. Y'know, lately, the last three, four years I been having trouble . . . "

"His name is Bart Templeton," the harness maker said. "Decent feller. Works hard, pays on the barrelhead, turns out good horses."

Alex tooled the team a short half mile before stopping to rest them — their heads pointing southward away from the cold air coming from the high northward mountains; one of the last things any man who liked horses would wish on them was chest-founder.

15

The men stiffly climbed down to spring their knees a little. The sun was climbing now. This large, grassy plateau was part of a heavily-timbered and black-shadowed series of stair-stepped serrated mountains which culminated about a hundred miles away, up where dirty snow lay year-round in the form of glacial ice among the crevices of granite rims and peaks.

While Foster and Abel stamped around, walked a little, Alex remained with his big horses adjusting straps, talking to the animals, making sure there were no galled places from traces or collars.

When Abel and Foster returned, they mentioned fresh wild-horse signs out yonder, and Alex, always protective of his team, scowled. "Remember a couple of years back when we come up here and that damned roman-nosed, coon-footed, rump-spring stud come nosin' around tryin' to pick a fight?"

They remembered; they'd had to talk like a pair of Dutch uncles to prevent irate Alex Smith from shooting the wild stallion.

"It'll be him again, sure as hell," Alex said rolling his one eye around the vastness of the grassy plateau. "Let's get across to the timber and set up camp."

Driving across the big meadow was a pleasure. Alex did not yank on the lines when his horses shot their heads out for slack, then snatched a mouthful of grass-heads. He never used a check-rein. When someone reproached him for babying his big horses, he would explain that they were the children, the family he didn't have. But he did not spoil them; they obeyed, were tractable, and seemed to like their owner.

There were birds nesting in the tall grass. Once the men started up a dog-coyote. He did not even look back. They could have shot him, they had belt guns as well as Winchesters; but it was a magnificent day, bell-clear, fragrant, and they were not cowmen — who shot coyotes on sight — so they sat watching until he disappeared far ahead in the timber.

They studied the darkly majestic stands of timber with their spike-needled tops, looking for those that had no needles and were a uniform weathered gray color. Snags. Standing dead trees.

It was getting warmer, so they shed their coats. As the big horses sweated, some crows appeared, raffish, noisy birds that circled the wagon and raucously scolded its passengers for being up where two-legged things were neither common nor welcome.

It took hours to cross the meadow. They saw more fresh wild-horse sign. They also had their attention brought to a gnawed deer carcass when both big horses snorted and edged far out and around the smell of death.

Abel leaned to expectorate and squinted. "Not too old a kill," he remarked. "I'd say a bear done it."

They came into shade finally, over near the creek which angled southwesterly for a mile before emerging from the forest to meander down across the plateau.

Making camp was a simple chore. Finding exactly the right place, though, would have required more time if they had not used the same site for a number of years.

Everything made of leather that had salt from horse sweat was pulled high into the trees and tied there. Even then porcupines and other varmints would try to get to it.

Their old stone ring was pretty well intact. They rearranged the stones, tossed down their bedrolls, draped booted Winchesters from low fir limbs, put their grub box and personal saddlebags close to the bedrolls, turned the big horses loose even though Alex had brought along two sets of army chain-hobbles. His horses never wandered. At least they never had, but Foster was gently putting aside his croaker sack, and scowling. But he said nothing. Where those big bay horses were concerned, trying to talk sense to Alex was like spitting against the tide.

Abel off-loaded the sack-wrapped coal oil bottle, the big crosscut saws, the wedges, mauls, and trimming axes. While the other two fussed at preparing a meal, Abel sat on an ancient deadfall examining the saw teeth.

If Alex was an old granny about his horses, Abel Morrison was a crank about saw teeth. He hadn't always been. He was crowding seventy. At thirty or even forty, a man could bull a dull crosscut through trees. After that, with reason to conserve his strength — unless he enjoyed exhaustion and a sore back — he got exactly the right 'set' when he filed and dressed saw teeth.

Foster stood erect by the nearly smokeless dry-wood fire and took down a big breath, noisily exhaled, and smiled widely. "I never envied In'ians," he said to no one in particular, his eyes bright, "but livin' in country like this, huntin' when they was of a mind to, loafin' and makin' babies on full moon nights, bein' as free as the wind . . ."

He did not finish, just sank to one knee, still smiling, to help Alex with the cooking. Whenever Alex had to squint his good eye against shifting tendrils of heat or smoke, he was blind as a bat.

Abel looked up from wiping the saws with coal oil. Like Alex Smith, Abel was woman-

19

less. Foster had never been married. "The huntin' and loafin' is fine, but I'll tell you something about makin' babies," he said quietly. "There's some kind of natural law about that."

Foster chuckled.

Abel ignored him and said, "Makin' them is pleasurable. But every damned heartache you get for the rest of your life, you get from your children."

Neither of the men looked around or pursued this topic. It was the first time they had ever heard Abel even hint that he'd had children.

CHAPTER 2
SOMETHING UNEXPECTED

The first fir snag was uphill a half mile from camp. They brought it down without snapping it in the middle, put the team on it, and skidded it to within a stone's throw of camp.

Over the years they had developed a system. Abel and Alex started the cut; then Foster took over from Abel. Foster and Abel took turns on one end of the saw and Alex, who was as strong as a bull, worked the opposite end. Alex's problem was that while he could see reasonably well, with one eye, he could not for some reason get a saw started straight. Foster had a bad back so he could run the saw for only short periods. Abel, with a bad heart, spelled Foster until his chest felt tight. Then he'd signal and Foster would take over again, while upon the far side of the big deadfall Alex would buck the saw, head down, red-faced and lips pursed.

The splitting was accomplished roughly the

same way, but in a more leisurely fashion so that neither Abel's chest nor Foster's bad back created problems. Not, that is, until they were finished for the day and went down to make a supper fire. Then Foster's back would give him hell, so Alex and Abel cooked and did most of the chores.

After nightfall, full and relaxed, they passed the bottle back and forth. Foster was lying flat out on the ground, when he laughed for no particular reason, propped himself up, and looking at his companions, said, "If some stranger was to come onto us workin', he'd sure wonder. A one-eyed man tryin' to hold a saw straight through a log, another feller lookin' peaked after runnin' one end of the saw ten minutes, and the third feller unable to straighten up after sunset."

Alex's eye twinkled by firelight. "If a man had a one-eyed horse, another one busted down in the back, an' still another one that'd fall down if he was run hard for a quarter mile — he'd shoot the lot."

Abel sprayed tobacco juice and listened to it hiss in the fire. "All we need is a one-legged man. Did I ever tell you boys about an old man I knew back in Missouri named Jeff Evinrude?"

Alex looked at Foster Bullard, then back. "Well, not this trip you haven't, Abel."

Abel said no more.

Alex fed broken limbs from the snag into their fire. It blazed up blue-hot and smoke-less. From his flat-out position looking up, Foster said, "I wish I'd remembered to bring along my mouth harp."

Alex had to tip his hat down to shut out some of the heat. "It don't matter that you forgot it," he said. "There'll be yappin' coy-otes tonight which amounts to the same thing. I can't tell them from your harmonica."

Abel had raised his head. He was peering beyond their firelight in the direction Alex had taken the big horses to graze. He sat motionless for a long moment before speaking softly. "Somethin' out there, over by the horses. Listen."

Alex didn't listen. He came up off the ground as though he had been sitting on a coiled spring. He had his Winchester in hand as he turned away from the firelight.

Foster sat up painfully, watched Alex Smith fade out in the moonless night, and turned finally toward Abel. "What did it sound like? I didn't hear anything."

Abel was peering out into the night, and listening, so he did not reply.

A solitary gunshot brought Foster Bullard up off the ground as though his back was as sound as new money. He covered the distance

23

to his saddleboot in three strides and yanked out the Winchester.

When he wanted to, bull-built Abel Morrison could move very fast for a man with a bad heart. He was already striding in the direction of the gunshot, carbine in hand, by the time Foster got untracked.

When they reached a small grassy place where the horses had been, they found neither the horses nor Alex. While Foster looked for sign, his companion leaned on his carbine trying to detect sounds. If they had been out in the open, he might have been more successful. But in among big trees where no grass grew among the layers of resin-impregnated fir needles, sounds were so effectively muffled they did not carry a hundred feet.

It was a moonless night, which made it nearly impossible for Foster to find tracks. This condition was also compounded by the fact that in among forest giants, starlight could not penetrate very well; even eighteen-hundred-pound draft horses with hooves like dinner plates would be hard to track. Foster was a stubborn man, though. Where it was necessary, he got down on all fours and groped over indentations with his fingers. Eventually he arose, brushed himself off, and went over to where Abel was straightening up with his carbine in the crook of his left arm. Foster pointed. "Damned horses been trampin' around here for several hours. Even in daylight, it'd be hard to read their sign. but the only marks I found headin' out of here went in that direction: southerly."

Abel nodded while fumbling for his plug. After he had a cud in place, he said, "Somethin' spooked them. Most likely a bear or a cougar. I told Alex fifty times to hobble his damned horses."

Foster waited until the anger was spent before quietly saying, "Abel, it's dark. It's late at night. There's no cougar or bear on earth hunts in the dark when he can't see."

Abel spat, eyeing Foster irritably. Of course Foster was right, but Abel did not admit it. He simply jerked his head and started walking.

Fifteen minutes later they were down at the timber stand that bordered the open grassland, and even without a moon they could see a fair distance out over a tundra of ghostly soft tan. Foster said, "Nothing. But they couldn't just disappear."

Abel held up his hand for silence. Moments later both men heard horses far southward. The rhythm of the echoes was not that of thousand-pound saddle animals; it was more like the rocking-chair, heavy stride of very large draft horses. It rose and fell with the clumsy awkwardness of big animals who were unaccustomed to running.

Foster pushed ahead and Abel caught his arm. Once they abandoned the timber they would have no background protection. "Let's just figure for a minute," he told Foster. "Now then, if it wasn't a varmint of some kind that run off Alex's horses, what was it?"

Foster brightened. "Wild horses. Sure as hell they picked up the scent a long time ago, maybe before sundown. A stallion came skulking around, spooked Alex's horses, and they're still running."

Abel grounded his Winchester as he sighed. "Then how's it come we can only hear the big horses? If that was a wild stud out there bitin' their rumps as he kept 'em going, how come he's not makin' any noise — and where in hell is Alex?"

Foster had no answer, but standing close to the trees as the echoes diminished irritated him. "You hang back an' ponder," he said shortly. "I'm goin ahead. If we lose those horses, we might just as well abandon everything and start walking."

Abel did not hang back. As they spread out and walked away from the forest, he strained to catch an occasional echo. It appeared that Alex's big horses were heading for the trail they had come up on earlier that day.

. What mystified them both was that the draft horses were still running. That certainly was not common with horses that large and heavy; for that matter, it wasn't common even among much lighter, more active and agile saddle animals. It did not take much to panic horses, but, with the exception of wild ones, they ordinarily did not run in fear any farther than they had to, which was perhaps about a mile or less. Unless, of course, they were being pursued, and Abel had been unable to pick up any sound to make him believe this was the case.

And where in the hell was Alex? In broad daylight he could not judge distance very well. In darkness, assuming there might be some kind of peril, one-eyed Alexander Smith would be at a terrible disadvantage, Winchester or no Winchester.

Foster sashayed to keep his course set according to the distinguishable marks and trampled tall grass left by the big horses. Only once did he beckon Alex over. That was when Foster had picked up a knitted cap. It was pale blue everywhere except where it had been turned up around someone's ears and forehead. Abel examined the thing and handed it back. "Hasn't been lyin' here very long, Foster, or mice would have been to work on it. They like wool awful well."

27

Foster turned the knit cap in his hands. He stretched it, turned it inside out, then wagged his head. "Right smack-dab in the tracks." He gazed at Abel as he punched the wool cap into a rear pocket. "They don't fall off easy, if a man's got the sense to pull 'em down low . . . This feller was too busy stealin' two big horses to bother with his cap."

Abel stood gazing southward for a long while before he spoke again. "It's hard to believe, Foster. I had some such idea back yonder, but it just seemed, well, unlikely as hell."

Foster was getting impatient again. "We can make better time out here in the open." He started forward as Abel made a dry remark.

"Foster, have you ever gone after horse thieves before? Because if you haven't, let me tell you that us two are out here in the open, an' even in the poor light if he's watchin' up yonder for pursuers, he's goin' to catch sight of us eventually. An' lying in the grass like an In'ian, he won't even have to shoot; he can just lie there until we walk up, then throw down on us."

Carbine held by the barrel over his shoulder, Foster kept right on walking, his full attention southward. Abel wagged his head and followed, maintaining the little distance between them.

They could no longer hear the big horses. In fact, they heard nothing at all, and that made Abel uneasy. He swung his head from left to right like an old sow bear.

Ordinarily Foster Bullard was unable to walk for any considerable distance, but tonight, with a chill creeping into the late night, he only occasionally glanced over where Abel was trudging along and did not once appear to be slackening his stride.

Far back a wolf sounded. Both men halted and turned. After a while, the wolf sounded again. Abel grounded his Winchester, chewed as he squinted up their backtrail, and said, "I'll be damned to hell."

Foster twisted to look southward, then gave it up with a shrug and sank to one knee in the grass leaning on his carbine. He had been astonished, but that was momentary. Now he was grinning. Foster never sulked; by nature he was even-tempered. "We must have walked right past him," he said.

"An why didn't the old fool make his bad wolf call then?"

They started back. When they met Alex Smith, both Foster and Abel were so relieved they did not complain; they just sank down on the ground, guns across their laps, and listened to what their companion had to tell them.

"I saw him," said Alex. "He was havin' one hell of a time tryin' to spring from the ground onto the back of one of the horses. He fell twice and got up to try again when I whistled, then fired. That time he went up and almost over. He had the other horse on a shank and busted out through the trees ridin' so low I couldn't risk another shot for fear of hittin' the horse."

Foster tugged at the knit cap, tossed it over in front of Alex, and said, "Was he wearing that thing?"

Alex held up the hat for better light, then lowered it "Yes. Where did you find it?"

Foster gestured vaguely. "Back down yonder a ways . . . He's still goin' south, Alex. If we got any hope of gettin' your horses back, we better quit sittin' here and cover ground."

Abel raised a hand. "I'll track him. You two head on back to camp. If no one is up there for a couple of days, we'll lose more than the horses; varmints will eat everything we got, ruin our harnesses, chew holes in everything with the smell of salt-sweat on it, gnaw off the saw handles . . . You two go back. Don't worry about me. I been in worse situations than this lots of times. If he goes anywhere near town with those horses, I'll get some help an' run him down on horseback."

Alex said, "An' hang the son of a bitch, Abel."

As Abel walked away he squinted ahead, but visibility was limited. He did not have much hope of seeing Alex's horses before sunrise, if then. What he had in mind was to track them if he could until he was down off the plateau, then angle toward town and round up some riders. He was confident about finding them once he was on horseback. In broad daylight those two big horses would leave tracks a child could follow.

He settled into an easy stride. Walking never seemed to bring on the chest-ache that bucking a cross-cut saw, or other form of strenuous upper-body activity did. In fact old Abel Morrison could walk a hole in the daylight; he had been doing it for more years than he liked to think about. He went often for long walks during good weather after he locked up the harness shop for the day. He liked to walk.

He was about midway across the big meadow when he suddenly laughed at the image of one-eyed Alex trying to shoot an agile horse thief in a damned forest in the dark. It was a miracle that he hadn't hit one of his horses.

With plenty of time to speculate, he thought about a number of things. One of them was that knitted cap. It was springtime, not winter, which was the wrong time of year for a man to be wearing that kind of a cap unless he did not have anything else. And what was the horse thief doing up yonder? As far as Abel knew, no one had lived on the mesa since the Indians were rounded up and taken away, years ago.

One thing seemed clear; the thief had probably watched them drive across the meadow from a hiding place back in the forest. He must have also spied on them as they set up camp and went to work. Unless he was already a fugitive, or unless he'd already made up his mind to steal the horses before Abel and his friends had established their camp, the normal thing for a man to do was walk into camp, eat supper, and visit. Loners in country like the big plateau usually were glad for company.

Even fugitives. In his earlier years Abel had occasionally encountered lonely men, some of whom he had been certain were hiding out. He had in fact spent some pleasant hours in the company of such men.

This one had a good reason for staying away. He had planned to steal Alex's big horses.

It was turning cold. Abel studied the sky. Dawn was on the way. He was almost to the wagon ruts. If daylight arrived before he started down, he would probably be able to see the thief and the big horses.

CHAPTER 3
TOWARD DAWN

Foster and Alex stirred up the fire, set the coffee pot in place, and sat glumly waiting. When the coffee was hot each man laced his cupful with whiskey.

It was colder among the big trees than it was out in the meadow.

Foster did not use tobacco but Alex did. He rolled a cigarette, lit it from the fire, blew smoke upwards, and sipped from his coffee cup before speaking.

"You don't expect he followed us up here, do you?" Foster asked.

Alex did not think so. "We'd have seen him behind us when we drove across the meadow. Naw, I'd say he was already up here and watched us arrive." He sipped laced coffee and squinted. "I purposeful shot high, Foster. I hoped it'd scare him, but it didn't. It was dark as hell among them trees."

Foster was sympathetic without saying so. "Come daylight we'd ought to scout a little.

34

He had to have a camp. What did he look like?"

"About like everyone else, I guess. I told you, it was dark among them damned trees." Alex sipped and relaxed a little; the whiskey was doing its work. "He tried to jump astraddle. He jumped like a man with rubber legs. Bounced up off the ground. He was in a hurry. Maybe if I hadn't shot, he wouldn't have been able to mount up. That gunshot acted like a physic; that son of a bitch come up off the ground with a jump you wouldn't believe. Like someone gave him one hell of a boost. He darned near sailed up and over the other side."

Foster considered the bottom of his empty cup. "Abel will catch him."

Alex was squinting into the fire. "Yeah. Once he gets a horse under him in town, he'll catch him. Only it bothers me to think of someone abusin' my horses, ridin' 'em too hard and all . . . I wish I'd been able to get a sighting on him when he wasn't right next to one of my animals. I'd have blowed him to kingdom come."

Foster did not refill his cup. He was tired. Even before the long walk he had been tired. All three of them had put in an arduous day. Abel, out there somewhere hiking along, was the oldest. He was seventy. Alex at sixty-five was the youngest. Foster was sixty-eight, but the fact was that men between the ages of sixty-five and seventy did not have any junior or senior status; they were just plain old.

Alex refilled his cup with black java and whiskey and without raising his face from the fire he said, "I must have had fifteen chances to sell them horses ... Pour some more in your cup, Foster ... When I bought them horses they was galled an' wormy and bony as hat racks. I must've been asked a hunnert times why a gunsmith who lives in town an' has got no reason to own horses bought them two." Alex's one eye rose to his friend's face across the fire. "That's pretty fair whiskey, Foster, for a fact."

"Yeah ... Why did you buy them?"

Alex dropped his head again. "I'm commencing to feel better. Why? They needed a friend real bad ... I ... a long time ago I had two little boys. I was freightin' back then. Sometimes I'd be gone a month or more ... You better fill your cup or there won't be none left Foster ... Anyways, I was gone seven weeks and come back to an empty house. Gone. Plumb gone. My wife and my little boys."

"Where did they go?"

Alex shrugged, cleared his pipes, and spat lustily into the fire. "Never found out where they went. Not a word. Those boys is about twenty, twenty-five years old by now." The solitary eye came up again. "Why don't they come, Foster?"

Foster was shaken and very uncomfortable. He had never heard a word of this before. All he knew was that Alex had said he was a widower. Well, in a way he was.

"Why, Foster?" Alex asked again.

"Maybe they don't know where you are, Alex. Maybe they can't trace you. How many Alex Smith's do you reckon there might be in the world?"

Alex drained his cup and pitched it aside. "Yeah, maybe. And maybe something else. Maybe their mother made gawddamned sure they'd never be able to find me."

"Aw, a woman wouldn't do that."

Alex made a faint death's-head smile. "Naw, a woman wouldn't do something like that . . . We was talkin' about my horses. I guess I needed them as much as they needed me. One's named Ned for my oldest boy. The other one's named Bugler for my youngest boy."

Foster had not refilled his cup and surreptitiously put it aside. "You named your youngest son Bugler?"

"No. What'n hell kind of a thing would that be to do a little boy? His name was Henry.

One time I brought him back an army bugle I traded for. He liked to drove everyone crazy learnin' to blow that thing. We started calling him Bugler ... Foster, I got to bed down, that damned whiskey sure went to work on me." As Alex arose unsteadily to head for his bedroll he said, "I got to have my horses back."

Foster watched Alex feel along his bedroll for the opening. "You'll get 'em back."

Foster, who had been drowsy a half hour earlier, was no longer drowsy. He and Alex Smith had been friends for many years and this was the first time during all their shared experiences Alex had ever talked about his personal life. He'd said he was a widower, so that was what Foster had believed, and right now as he sat hunched before the dying fire he wished they had never put that damned whiskey in their coffee on empty stomachs. Foster made a serious business of being good-natured. He'd had to, otherwise between his dissolving lower spine and the ivory teeth that were the source of continual discomfort when he ate — and a source of embarrassment when they dropped loose, especially the upper ones, during conversations — he could very easily have become bitter, mean, and cranky. He'd seen it happen with other men with disabilities, and he had made up his mind long ago that he'd be damned if he'd let that happen to him.

Right now, though, staring into the fire and listening to Alex snoring, he just simply could not raise his spirits, so he went off to his blankets, too, leaving the fire to dwindle to pink coals just before dawn arrived.

It had been a long night, one that none of them could have anticipated or even imagined. When gray dawn stealthily arrived Foster and Alex slept on, blissfully unaware that an old boar bear had picked up the camp scent from a half mile back up through the timber. Moving intuitively without haste, the bear had arrived at the site of the deadfall snag the men had been working on as the sky faintly brightened. He was sitting up there now, making a dim-witted predator's evaluation of what lay below him.

One of the bear's ears was halfway gone, testimony to a fierce battle he no longer remembered. He also had a milky cast over one eye which was the result of a raking lion claw during another battle.

He was scarred and arthritic. It had been a long time since he'd been able to run down prey. Long guard-hairs on his underside meant he had belly worms. He smelled of the carrion he'd been reduced to living off of for several years, and he had not been without hunger pains for a long time. But his sense of smell was still very good. He wrinkled his nose at the smell of food coming from the boxes and saddlebags lying close to the dying fire.

He knew man-smell. He had encountered men before. He had a severed tendon from a glancing bullet that made his gait even more awkward than it normally would have been.

The bear sat for a long time, moving his head slightly in an effort to determine exactly where the food was. In his prime he had feared nothing, not even men with rifles. He still feared nothing as he raised up on his hind legs and swayed a little. The food aroma did not seem to come from one particular place, which meant he would have to rummage the entire camp.

As he eased back down onto all fours, one of the bedrolls shifted and a man-sound came from it, like a cross between a snore and a cough, which was a sound not unlike his own garrulous snufflings. He watched that particular bedroll with his one good eye, then started ambling toward it. He roughly cuffed a round of unsplit snag wood aside and barged ahead. The round rolled toward the camp, gathering downhill momentum. It bounced off a fir tree, slewed sideways and tumbled ahead, struck the stone cooking ring, rolled up over it, and landed in the hot ash. Coals beneath the round seared woodpecker holes until the acorns stored in the holes began exploding.

Foster opened both eyes wide awake, waited a moment listening to the popping sounds, then eased up very slowly and saw the old bear swaying in an ungainly amble directly toward Alex's bedroll. For three seconds he was too petrified to even breathe; then he jerked clear of his blankets reaching for the Winchester three feet away.

He was on the bear's blind side, but when he rolled to get the carbine the bear heard him moving and paused, rocked back, and began to push upright as he turned his head from side to side.

Foster froze. He would not have time to raise the gun, cock and aim it before the bear saw movement, so he became rigid. The old bear sensed danger and stood up to his full height swaying from side to side. He could not retreat. Even if that idea had occurred to him, he had committed himself to a course of action that would, hopefully, lessen the hunger agony in his belly. That was the only thought in his brain.

His eyesight was poor. Even if he had not had the filminess over one eye he still would not have possessed good eyesight. He hunted

41

by scent and movement, not by visual contact.

Foster was white to the hairline waiting for the boar bear to drop back down on all fours and turn away.

Another grunt of coughing came from Alex's bedroll. The bear wrinkled his nose and turned away from Foster. Alex moved sluggishly in the blankets. The bear put his flat head close to the ground sniffing.

Foster very gently snugged back the carbine, rested a thumb on the hammer, and held his breath because the moment he cocked the gun that bear would hear the sound and turn on him.

Foster had never shot a bear before in his life, but he had listened to a great many men who had, and of all their stories he remembered one thing: Shooting a bear head-on against his very thick, sloping skull, would only bring down one bear out of a dozen.

He lowered the barrel a fraction. If the bear had been sideways, he could have tried a heart shot directly behind the shoulder. But the bear was not sideways to him, so he pushed the blankets away with his stocking feet and came up very slowly until he was in a high crouch. The bear was beside Alex's bedroll now, pushing gently at the blankets with one front paw. He began making the guttural, complaining sounds typical of his kind.

Foster thought he saw Alex stiffen in his blankets, but if he had indeed done that, it was all he did as Foster's spine flamed with pain because of his slightly forward crouch. He locked the ivory teeth hard together and ventured two steps sideways. The bear was pawing Alex's bedroll again, concerned only with what he was doing.

Foster took two more steps sideways, stepped on a sharp stone in his stocking feet, ground his teeth then took two more steps.

He had a good sighting of the boar bear's right side at the shoulder, and slightly behind the shoulder. Sweat made his palms slippery as he knelt, fought off the pain, took careful aim, and cocked the gun. The bear's head came around instantly.

Foster fired, levered up and fired again, levered up and fired a third time. He did not raise his eyes from the gunsights until after that third shot.

The old bear was sitting back on his haunches looking squarely at the man who had shot him. He was capable of absorbing the impact without flinching.

Foster had salt-sweat stinging his eyes as he methodically levered up his fourth bullet. The bear coughed once; blood mixed with saliva spilled down his front.

Alex shot out of his bedroll like the seed being popped out of a grape. He did not even look back until he was behind a fir tree, then he yelled, "The throat! Shoot him in the throat!"

Foster shouldered the carbine, blinked at the sweat, and pulled down a deep, shaky breath.

The old boar bear turned to swing down onto all fours and did not make it; his legs folded beneath him, letting the foul-smelling, mangy coated body settle to the ground without even raising dust. The bear's head sank forward on both front paws, the good eye and the milky one looking blankly up the hill in the direction of the butchered fir snag.

Alex came cautiously from behind his tree, and flinched the moment his stocking-feet encountered a very small spiny fir cone.

Foster sat down on the ground holding the Winchester in his lap. He did not hear a high, far-away shout back down across the big meadow behind him. He did not even hear Alex speak from beside the bear where Alex was gingerly poking the carcass with a long stick, poised for flight if there was any reaction.

"I was sleepin' like a log . . . Jesus but he stinks . . . How the hell did you know he was over here? Foster, are you all right. Jest set there, I'll get one of those bottles of whiskey. Just set there."

CHAPTER 4
A BAD MORNING

They drank cold whiskey on empty bellies and watched with puffy eyes as a considerable cavalcade approached from far out across the meadow. Alex rubbed his eye and tipped his head to squint harder. "Foster? Is that my big horses them folks are leading?"

Foster had his back resolutely to the dead bear when he replied. "Looks like it, looks like it for a fact. I'll bet new money on it, Alex. There aren't no other horses that big in the country, that I know of."

Alex lowered his face but still squinted. "How many do you make?"

Foster counted. "Four on horseback." He leaned slightly. "Tell you what I think, Alex. You see that feller in the drag leading the big horses: that'll be Abel."

"Who are the others?"

Foster did not reply for a full two minutes, by which time the riders were closer. "I'll tell you who two of them is — that horsebreaker who married John Holbrook's girl last year."

"Templeton," stated Alex. "Bart Temple-ton."

Foster nodded. "Bart Templeton. The one ridin' beside him sure as hell is a woman — unless maybe it's a man with a couple of apples in his shirt-pockets. Alex, by golly that's John Holbrook's daughter. What's her name?"

"Nan. It was Nan Holbrook. Now it's Nan Templeton." Alex ran a rough hand over his stubbly face. He did not share Foster Bullard's surprise about the woman. Foster stood staring as he said, "Why would a man bring his wife up to a place like this?"

Alex was becoming annoyed. "Why wouldn't a man do that? She's almost as handy with livestock as her husband. She's been her pa's eyes an' ears since she was in pigtails."

Both men got to their feet. Alex was finally able to distinguish individual riders. He scowled. "Who is ridin' that leggy bay horse — he's bareback ain't he?"

For a while Foster stared before he gradually stiffened. "It's an In'ian," he exclaimed. "Alex, he's wearin' an old sweater the same color as that knit cap we found. I'll lay you big odds he's the feller stole your horses."

Alex remained standing, his leathery dark face getting grimmer by the moment as Foster

47

knelt at the stone ring to start a fire. The visitors would need hot coffee and something to stick to their ribs.

Aside from being glad about the horses, Foster was enormously relieved at having visitors. He went to the creek to scrub, then returned to arrange the iron fry pans for cooking. He did not even once look around at the dead bear.

The lead horseman raised his gloved right hand. Alex did the same but not enthusiastically, and when the riders came up and swung off, Bart Templeton, a handsome, lanky man accumulating gray at the temples, gestured back where Abel Morrison was untangling lead shanks to Alex's two big horses. "Brought your friends back," he said, and was turning toward his wife when Alex fixed his eye upon the fourth member of the party.

"Who is he?" Alex asked darkly. "We got a knit cap that matches his sweater."

Templeton paused, then turned back. Abel was walking up leading the draft animals, and he spoke before Templeton had an opportunity to. As he passed over the lead ropes, Abel said, "That there is Jumping Mouse. He's a Shoshoni-Piute. That's what he told us."

Alex's eye did not waver from the Indian's face. He was not interested in anything Abel had said. "Shoshoni-Piute! I don't care if he's

48

King Solomon: did he steal my horses?"

Abel accepted a tin cup of hot coffee from Foster and winked. Foster did not wink back; he turned quickly to fill other cups.

Abel blew on the coffee because it was hotter than original sin. He eyed Alex over the cup's rim. "He's sixteen years old an' got no family. He's been livin' off squirrels and whatever else he could snare up in here since his folks an' a lot of other In'ians died from the cholera on the reservation up north where he was born."

Alex refused a cup of coffee from Foster and put his eye upon Abel as he said, "Did he steal my horses? That's all I want to know."

For a long while there was not a sound except for the crackling of Foster's breakfast fire, not until Abel Morrison tasted his coffee, swallowed, then said, "Yes." Alex moved in the direction of his bedroll and the dead bear. His Winchester was over there. The Indian, standing beside the horse he had been riding, dropped the reins and hurled around to flee. He ran into Bart Templeton's open arms, and although he struggled desperately he was unable to break away.

Alex glared as he straightened around holding the carbine. Abel was blocking his view of the struggling Indian. Abel looked directly at Alex and sipped coffee. Alex snarled at him.

"Get out of the way!"

Foster arose slowly from beside the stone ring. "Alex, what d'you think you're doing?"

"I'm going to settle with a horse thief, that's what I'm doing. Stand aside, Abel."

Abel continued to sip coffee without saying a word, but his gaze never left Alex Smith's face.

Alex raised the carbine. "Abel, get the hell out from in front of me."

Abel lowered the empty cup. "You are makin' a damned fool of yourself," he told the one-eyed man quietly. "What's Miz Templeton goin' to think, the way you're acting an' all?"

Alex's breath whistled out. "Are you goin' to get out'n the way, Abel?"

Foster's ivory teeth were showing through a ghastly smile. "Alex, if it wasn't for me you wouldn't even be here. You wouldn't have got your damned horses back. If I'd run into the trees like you done, that bear would have strung your guts out for a hundred feet . . . *Put down that gun!*" Foster's tongue made a darting circuit of his lips. "Alex — you owe me an' you know it! Now put that gun down or you're goin' to have to shoot your way through me'n Bart both . . . *Put it down!*"

No one moved or made a sound; every eye was on Abel's livid face.

Nan Templeton moved to the stone ring, leaned to fill a tin cup, straightened up, and walked in front of Abel. She stopped six inches from the Winchester barrel and held out the cup. "Please," she said, then waited.

Alex's mouth loosened, his expression of righteous wrath faded slightly, and he lowered the carbine, turning it aside as he did so. He was beginning to feel slightly ill. That was the only time in his sixty-five years he'd held a gun that was pointing at a woman.

He let the Winchester fall and accepted the cup of coffee. Abel turned aside, saw the rigid expression on Foster's face, and lightly slapped him on the back as he said, "You're goin' to burn the hoecakes."

Bart Templeton still held the Indian youth, but not as tightly because the Indian was no longer struggling. He felt limp in Templeton's arms. Bart leaned and said, "Go sit by the fire; get something to eat. And don't try to run again."

The youth obeyed but approached the fire ring from the west side. Alex was standing on the east side. As the Indian squatted, he did not take his eyes off the darkly tanned man with the white cloth patch where his left eye should have been.

While the others stood around the stone ring, Alex walked over to his horses, went

51

over each one meticulously by hand, then led them out where the feed was strong. At the fire Abel Morrison shook his head because even now Alex did not put hobbles on the animals.

Alex remained out with horses until Foster filled a tin plate and took it out to him. As he squatted beside Alex he said, "I told you last night you'd get them back."

Alex, with his back to the fire ring, gulped food and growled around it. "A horse thief is a horse thief and you know it. Don't matter if he's sixteen an' an orphan or sixty with ten kids."

Foster worked up a smile. "Alex, they are horses. Nice, big stout handsome ones for a fact, but they're still horses. They're not Ned and Bugler. I'll go get you a cup of java."

"Wait. I'll get my own coffee." Alex would not meet his old friend's gaze, he chewed and squinted southward out across the plateau and changed the subject. "What's Templeton doin' up here?"

"He come up to scout for wild horses, him and his missus. They was ridin' up with two pack horses an' saw the In'ian boy ridin' your horses. The horses was tired. They split up an' come in on him from both sides. They didn't have much trouble. He didn't even have a decent knife . . . They was on their way up here anyway an' they could tell by the tracks this was where your horses had come from, so they started along — and come onto Abel. They left both pack outfits down yonder, put Abel on one horse, the boy on the other one, and come up here . . . They got to go back shortly and get the packs before varmints find them and tear up everything."

Alex finally turned his head, just a little, just enough for his right eye to see Foster's face. "I wasn't runnin' into the timber to hide. That bear was square astraddle of both my guns. There wasn't anythin' else I could do."

Foster continued to smile. "Yeah, I know. I didn't mean you run because you was scairt."

The solitary dark eye remained on Foster's face. "I was scairt pee-less. I've seen a lot of bears in my time, shot my share, but by gawd that's somethin' I never imagined: openin' my eye out of a sound sleep and there, less'n two feet from me, was that son of a bitch lookin' right down at me. I could smell his breath. Foster, for two or three seconds I couldn't even move."

Foster laughed softly, slapped Alex on the shoulder, and arose to return to the others. Alex said, "Wait . . . Abel was right, I looked pretty foolish, didn't I?"

"Well, you sure had everyone's attention, Alex."

"You know what those horses mean to me."

"Yes, I know. Now finish eatin' and come back. It's over and finished, like the damned bear is over and finished."

Alex twisted to look straight up. "You and Abel still want to stay here until we got a load of wood?"

"Hell yes," responded Foster. "That's what we come up here for, isn't it? One lousy old boar bear and a raggedy-pantsed, half-grown buck ain't goin' to change what we're here for."

Alex remained out with his horses until he had finished eating, then arose, and walked back with a self-conscious shamble.

Only the Indian boy still looked wary; the others acted as though nothing had happened. Foster began portioning out the food.

Later, they hitched the big horses to the bear carcass and dragged it away, and that was so much like a three-ring circus no one, including Alex, remembered the earlier bad moments.

Horses, even those weighing close to a ton, had not been endowed by Mother Nature to be valorous animals; that's why she gave them four legs and a stomach that was never bloated with enough feed to slow them in flight. They feared bears and mountain lions above the two-dozen or more other things they were afraid of, and this particular bear smelled overpoweringly bad, not just from boar bear scent, which was rank enough, but from carrion stench which arose from his carcass in the warm sunshine in nearly visible waves.

In order to get the horses anywhere near the carcass, the men had to fill the distance between with every length of chain and rope in the camp. Then Alex went up front and led the horses.

Abel went with him, chewing on a fresh cud and keeping an eye on the bloating carcass far back. When they were a fair distance out, where there was an unobstructed neck of open land leading into the timber, Abel suggested they make a big circle, cut loose up in there, and leave the bear for the scavenging critters. Alex agreed and led his horses up the slight incline. When they eventually cut loose and started back, Alex put a sidelong look on Abel and said, "That was a tomfool thing to do, Abel, get smack-dab in front of me."

Abel spat. "You wouldn't have yanked the trigger."

"Well, of course I wouldn't have — but if that In'ian had busted loose and run I couldn't have got a shot at him with you in front of me like you was."

Abel nodded, chewed, said nothing and continued to walk toward the distant camp.

Alex said no more either. They had settled something they both would like to forget.

With the camp in sight, Abel said, "Hell, Templeton and his wife are gone."

Alex peered from beneath his floppy hat-brim. "Probably went back down for their packs."

Abel nodded. "Yeah."

"Foster said they was on there way up here to look for wild horses."

"That's what he told me on the ride up here. Seems he's built a couple of salting traps a few miles eastward. He had some sacks of rock salt in his pack he figured to put out, then him and his wife figured to make a high camp where they can keep watch, and come back later to do the real trapping."

Alex was interested. "By gawd, how many women did you ever know who'd do some-thin' like that with their man?"

Abel was squinting up ahead where Foster was cleaning up around the stone ring when he answered. "Just one, partner, just one, an' that was a long time ago, an' she died of lung fever," then he looked around and smiled gently. "Miz' Templeton's a looker. I remem-ber seein' her drive into Holtville with her paw years ago. Pretty as a speckled bird even then. Now . . . " Abel wagged his head as though he could not find suitable words to describe beautiful Nan Templeton.

Foster had the camp in order, but the smell of the bear remained, and would for several days. The three old men went over into the shade to sit for a spell. Enough had happened before the sun had reached its meridian to fill at least one full day, and while they discussed some aspects of it — not Alex's sudden blind rage or what had gone with it — the sun continued to move.

Abel finally stretched out in fir shade, punched his hat into a pillow and got comfortable as he said, "I must have walked five hundred miles last night. It was cold to boot. I'm goin' to sleep for a spell. If anything more crops up, like maybe a mountain lion this time, wake me."

Alex was looking down in the direction of the stone ring. "What do we do with the In'ian pup? I thought the Templetons would take him with them. Look at him; he's sitting down there like a stone. Why didn't he come up into the shade with us?"

"Because," said Abel drowsily, "he's scairt peeless of you."

"What are we going to do with him?"

Abel sighed loudly. "Put him to work makin' firewood tomorrow. Now will you shut up, please?"

Foster arose and jerked his head for Alex to

follow him as he walked back down to camp. The Indian youth was eating scraps he had hidden in his filthy old sweater and glanced up as they walked past. Alex put a flinty look downward but kept on walking.

They pulled the grub box back up into a tree and made several small piles of dry wood near the stone ring. They also went over to the creek to wash, and while he was kneeling over there Alex twisted to look back. The Indian youth was still chewing. He had not taken his eyes off them since they had walked back down from the shade. Alex bent forward to scoop water with cupped hands as he said, "Foster, don't it make you uneasy, him starin' at our backs?"

Foster was shaking off water as he replied. "No. His daddy, maybe, and sure as hell his grand-daddy, but not him. All he's got is a busted old rusty clasp knife."

Alex said no more until they were arising from the creekbank. "All right, we'll feed him in exchange for him helpin' us make wood — then what? Turn him loose up in here?"

Foster cleared his throat twice before answering. "We could do that, for a fact, an' maybe with summer comin' he could kill deer an' rabbits and whatnot, an' then again maybe he might break a leg or get sick."

The one good eye came around with a sulphurous glow. "No you don't, Foster Bullard. Not behind my horses, you don't take him back with us. No damned horse-stealin' mangy In'ian!"

CHAPTER 5
THE CAP LOG

They put in two strenuous days snaking down four more snags and working them into manageable lengths to be loaded on the running gear. Jumping Mouse worked as hard as any of them, and he never once in the two days volunteered a single word. He would answer a question or obey an order, but otherwise he might as well have been mute.

However, on one score he rated higher than the older men. When it came to eating, Jumping Mouse could outdo all three of them. Alex ruefully wagged his head. Abel was amused, and Foster was fascinated that anyone less than six feet tall and who looked to weigh no more than a hundred and forty pounds with rocks in his pockets, could hold so much food.

They did not begrudge him. They had brought along enough grub for ten days, and the way things looked now, they would be able to load logs and head out in another three days, so there would be grub left over. Moreover, although they had brought Winchesters along for the express purpose of getting camp meat if it was necessary, it did not seem to be something they would have to do, which would be a mild disappointment because all three of them liked to hunt.

After the second day of very hard physical labor, Foster had difficulty rolling out in the morning. His best effort to conceal the fact that he could not stand erect without gritting his teeth was noticed by Abel and Alex. They mentioned at breakfast that the two of them and Jumping Mouse could block-and-tackle the trimmed logs onto the running gear; Foster could help more by striking camp. Foster had to accept this because he could not even have walked back up to where the logs were lying ready to be loaded. But he was morose enough to lace his coffee, something he never did for breakfast.

Abel and Alex trudged back up where the work had been done trailed by Jumping Mouse, who as usual, said nothing, but when the matter of pulling on the chain-block made Abel's knees wobble, the Indian youth elbowed in to pull the chain in front of Abel, who gratefully went to sit down for a while. Alex and the youth strained, paused to rest, and resumed straining in absolute silence. Once a log was in place on the running gear,

Alex would use an arm-sized green fir limb to jockey it into position. It was hard work; they sweated and occasionally rested. During those times, Alex surreptitiously eyed the Indian, and shortly before noon when they went up into the shade to drink from their canteens and sit with their backs against trees, he finally said, "Boy, you speak English pretty well, do you?"

Jumping Mouse nodded his head and afterwards raised a hand to push his long hair back as he gave Alex a swift sidelong look.

Alex scratched, looked dourly at the half-loaded running gear and squinted his eye nearly closed. "Stealin' horses can get you hung, do you know that?"

The youth nodded again. He looked toward the wagon, too.

Alex reddened. "Listen to me. When someone talks to you, damn it answer back, don't just bob your head. You understand?"

Jumping Mouse squirmed a little where he was sitting. "I understand."

"Hmph! That's better. Now then, tell me why you tried to steal my horses."

The youth looked at the ground, took a long time to reply, and picked up a small stone to gaze at as he replied. "I wanted to go far south. One of the teachers at the reservation school showed us a map one time showing where the tribes were. I wanted to go south and find them. It is a very long way. On foot someone would have stopped me, maybe some sheriff or cattleman."

Alex plucked at a patch of pitch on one callused hand. "Why didn't you stay where you come from?"

"My parents died from a sickness. A lot of Indians died. I didn't want to die too. I left at night and walked."

"Walked from where?"

Jumping Mouse raised a ragged sleeve. "North, far to the north."

"All your folks is dead?"

"I had two brothers. They left the reservation a long time ago."

"Well, maybe them In'ians down south wouldn't want you. Did you think of that?"

"I had to take that chance because no one else would want me."

Alex continued to pick at the pitch. "You had a camp up in here?"

Again the youth gestured. "Up the same creek you get water from."

"What you been livin' on?"

"Berries. Sometimes I could catch some meat. Roots like I used to help my mother gather."

Alex raised his eye, still narrowed, to study the thinness of the boy. "No deer or wapiti?"

"No I tried snares, but the deer broke them."

Alex went back to picking pitch. "Where'd you get such a name as Jumpin' Mouse?"

"From my mother."

"Is that what they called you at the In'ian school?"

"No. They called me Jim Moore. They said it sounded better, but I like Jumping Mouse."

Alex raised his head to look around and blew out a big breath. "What do you figure to do after we finish makin' wood up here and head for home?"

"Go back to my camp."

"What if you busted a leg, or got sick from that stuff you eat?"

Jumping Mouse did not reply. Alex looked quickly at him then away, down toward camp where Foster was puttering noisily, then to their left where Abel was sound asleep and snoring in the fragrant shade. Jumping Mouse surprised him by asking a question.

"That lady named Templeton — is she Indian?"

Alex could not recall having heard much about Nan's mother, but he knew her father, who certainly had no Indian blood. He scowled as he replied. What caused him trouble was that Nan could have had Indian blood; she had some of the color for it. "I can't say. I don't know. Did you talk to her on the ride up here?"

"No. I didn't talk to any of them. She looks Indian."

Alex scoffed. "Naw, she don't. Not real In'ian."

" 'Breed-Indian," the boy said. "We had many of them on the reservation."

Alex had an uncomfortable feeling of having heard something about Nan's mother. He struggled to remember and failed. He said, "I don't know as it makes any difference."

Jumping Mouse started to arise. "Them logs won't climb onto the wagon by theirselves."

Alex sighed and grunted up to his feet. He and the boy walked about thirty feet when Alex stopped. "We better go down an' get something to eat. You go on ahead, I'll shake Abel awake."

The youth obediently walked away, Alex stood motionless watching him, then turned to go rouse Abel.

Foster had coffee and hoecakes waiting for them. His back was a little better but not a whole lot better. He sat on the ground with them and ate as he said, "I just remembered what they call this big plateau up here. Wild Horse Mesa."

Abel did not even look up from his tin

plate. Alex grunted. They both knew this.

Foster watched the youth eat and wagged his head. "You keep that up," he said, "an' you won't have no pleats in your belly for the rest of your life."

Alex's head came up. "He's earned it, Foster."

Both the other older men looked at Alex but said nothing.

Near the end of the meal one of the big horses raised his head gazing westward, and made a loud whinnying sound. Alex turned to stare as Foster said, "Most likely he picked up the scent of the Templetons' horses. Bart said him an' his wife was goin' to scout up the mesa. They could be up in the timber close by."

Alex went back to eating, finished, put his tin plate aside, and shoved upright to hitch at his britches and wait for Jumping Mouse to also arise. He then led the way back up where the logs were, and Abel, who hung back a little, watched Alex and the boy briefly, dropped a sly look to Foster and said, "He's got himself a mascot."

Foster shook his head. "No, he don't. He told me he wouldn't have no bronco ride back behind his horses with us."

Abel shrugged and walked away.

It was a hot afternoon, made more so by a

high veil that covered the sky, diffused sunlight, and added a noticeable breathlessness to the day.

"Rain weather," Alex said to Abel, who leaned on his trimming axe to look upward. "I hope it holds off until we're down off this meadow. If that road goin' down is wet, those big horses won't be able to hold back the load and using skid chains won't help much."

Jumping Mouse learned quickly. Either that or he'd loaded logs before. In either case, he knew how to set the tackle chain with just enough slack to give the pullers a fair start before they came up even with the log. He was also nimble and quick. He could disengage the chain choker quicker than Abel or Alex. Although he was careful, the older men continually cautioned him — not so much because he really needed to be warned of the deadly danger of loading logs, but because they were worried about him.

In midafternoon when the three of them trooped back over into shade to tank up and rest for a while, Abel grinned at the youth as he said, "Boy, you're wastin' your talents livin' in the Blue Mountains. You'd ought to go to work in town or maybe for one of the cow outfits."

The Indian seemed embarrassed by Abel's rough praise. As though to make less of his work he said, "I done this before, with my father and some of the old men. But we didn't have a very good chain-fall. The blocks was wood and they broke a lot."

"Did you split the logs before loading them, like we're doing?"

"No." The boy looked at Abel. "We should have, huh?"

"Makes 'em easier to handle, and they aren't as likely to roll back and maybe hurt a man."

Jumping Mouse said mockingly, "Dumb damned Indians."

Alex looked quickly at him. "No such a thing," he exclaimed. "If folks aren't showed the easy way to do things, how they are supposed to know?"

The sun was slanting away, which increased the shadows in the forest. It also made it a little cooler. Now, rising dust from the work was more noticeable, which it hadn't been during full daylight. To some extent the dust hindered visibility. Also, they had been working since early morning; they were getting tired and slower, their reflexes were no longer as quick as they had been during the morning.

Alex paused occasionally to wipe his eye. The dust bothered it a little.

They had leveled the load, which allowed for the positioning of two smaller, unsplit round logs on top, and one more final round log atop the lower two. That capped the load. They ratchetted the two lower logs into place; Alex grunted up to use his fir limb like a peavy, and left it between the logs to hold them slightly apart to make a good nesting place for the cap log.

Abel and Jumping Mouse watched from below, resting until Alex scrambled down, then Jumping Mouse leaned to warp each end of the last log high enough off the ground to get the chain under and around it. Alex and Abel evened up the chain and fastened it to the chain-blocks. Abel smiled and said to Alex, "This here is the log we been lookin' for since we started. The last one."

They had two sturdy saplings lying against the load for skids. Each sapling was chained to the wagon so that as the cap log was ratchetted upward, the skids would not move.

Alex spat on his callused hands and gripped chain. Abel moved behind him to do the same thing. Jumping Mouse looped a rope to one end of the log to keep it from turning right or left as it went up the skids.

Alex spoke over his shoulder. "You set, Abel?"

"Yep."

They began pulling on the chain. When the slack had been taken up and the log moved against the skids, Jumping Mouse watched closely because this was where it would twist if it was going to — and it did, so he sat back, waited until the log was off the ground, then pulled to straighten the log as it started up the skids.

Alex shook off sweat. The log was neither large nor particularly heavy in comparison to some of the other lengths they had loaded, but it had to go all the way up the side of the load and over. He and Abel had to work steadily. When the cap log was midway up the skids, which was about where they had been able to ease off on the other logs, it was still only halfway up. As Alex regripped the chain, his eye stung from sweat and his muscles bulged from strain but worked smoothly. He swore under his breath.

Jumping Mouse abruptly looked back because the log had stopped moving. He let out a curse he had certainly not learned at the reservation school.

Alex, his legs locked hard and his muscles bunched along his arms and shoulders, gasped at Jumping Mouse, "What is it?"

The youth's face was contorted. "Mister Morrison. He's sagging to his knees."

Abel's face was ashen, his lips had lost color. His legs were crumbling beneath him, but he stubbornly clung to the chain with

70

both hands. He had both eyes closed and breath was gusting past his lips.

Alex heard breath rattling behind him and stared whitely at Jumping Mouse. "Get out of the way," he croaked. "Get away, boy, I can't hold it."

The Indian dropped his rope. Instead of running, he leapt straight at Alex, whirled in front of him and locked both hands on the chain, which was beginning to pay back as Alex's strength waned.

"Damn you, get the hell away!" Alex croaked. He had used all the breath he could spare to say that.

Jumping Mouse was rigidly braced. "Let it slip slow," he said. "Slow."

The log began to slide back down. Jumping Mouse's neck was red from straining, his eyes did not leave the log as he allowed the chain to go through his hands inches at a time. Behind him Alex said, "Can't do it."

The youth strained harder, sweat poured off him, his jaw was locked. "You got to. Slower . . . "

It seemed to take a lifetime before the log came down the skids and bumped against the ground. Jumping Mouse risked a look back. Alex's mouth was wide open, his shirt was soaking wet. He met the Indian's stare with blurred vision. "Throw a kink in the chain,"

Alex gasped. The youth obeyed and as the chain could no longer pass through the blocks, effectively halting the log, Alex eased up very gradually. The kinked knot held.

Alex felt slack and let the chain fall. He waited until Jumping Mouse shoved a sawed round under the log, then he turned, chest on fire, lungs pumping, and slowly sat down.

Abel was lying on his face. If they had been unable to halt the log's descent it would have rolled over all of them, but especially Abel Morrison, who was unconscious.

Jumping Mouse ran for a canteen, handed it to Alex, who drank some water and doused what remained over Abel.

CHAPTER SIX
THE HEART OF THE MATTER

Foster struggled up to the loading site where he saw Alex easing Abel Morrison over onto his back. With a deeply furrowed brow, he leaned a little as he said, "Is he dead?"

Alex did not respond; he was loosening Morrison's neckerchief and putting his hat under Abel's head. The unconscious man had blue lips, and there was a hint of a bluish tint under his eyes.

Foster wrung his hands and made a little clicking sound with his ivory teeth. He looked around at the youth. "Boy, go fetch that bottle of whiskey settin' in the shade behind the grub box. Run, damn it!"

Jumping Mouse ran.

Alex sat back on his haunches. While looking at Abel's face he said, "Damned shallow breathing, and sort of fluttery . . . Foster, he had no business comin' up here. He ain't up to this sort of work."

73

Foster said, "It's his wagon."

Alex turned a fiery eye on Foster. It was such an inane statement to make. Of course it was his wagon, but what the hell did that have to do with Abel overdoing it just now?

Foster came closer and peered worriedly downward. Alex said, "Will you, for Chris'-sake, stop makin' that noise with your teeth!"

The little rattling noise stopped as Foster leaned down until his back shot a spasm of pain upwards; then he straightened up a little. "I'll get some water," he said. "Cool him off."

Alex ignored the departure of his friend and continued to sit back like an old squaw in mourning. He was irritable, sweaty, rumpled and very worried.

Jumping Mouse returned with the bottle, put it beside Alex, and moved to the opposite side of Abel Morrison. The youth dropped to both knees and, with Alex watching with a widening expression of bafflement, inserted a hollow dry reed into Abel's mouth, working it gently so far down Alex was about to snarl at him. Then the Indian leaned over, filled his lungs and blew steadily into the reed.

He continued to do this until Abel's fingers began to twitch.

Witnessing this, Alex exclaimed, "Gawddamn!"

Jumping Mouse raised his eyes and continued to work at the hollow reed. Abel's eyelids flickered, his nostrils flared, and finally he feebly raised an arm and with quivering fingers tried to brush something away — whatever was gagging him.

Jumping Mouse withdrew the reed and sat back, as Alex was doing, to watch.

Foster returned with a canteen full of water. He halted to watch as Able sucked down huge, slow inhalations of mountain air, both eyes open. Foster put the canteen down.

They were silent and still for a full ten minutes watching Abel Morrison struggle to recover. His color still did not improve much, and he was clearly too weak to move; but he was breathing, and occasional little twitches showed that his limbs had blood pumping to them again.

Alex slowly reached for the whiskey bottle. He drank from it and offered it to Foster, who also drank. Alex fished for a limp old faded blue bandana to mop his face and neck with, and as he was stowing the thing, he looked across Abel at Jumping Mouse. "Where'd you learn that trick?" he asked softly.

The youth stared at Abel's face when he answered. "From my mother. She told me she learnt it from her grandfather, who was a Navajo."

Foster, who had been down filling the canteen at the creek when Jumping Mouse revived Abel, did not know what they were talking about. But he did not ask; Alex did not seem to be in a mood to answer questions.

Alex finally trickled whiskey down Abel's gullet. Not much, and more was spilled than was swallowed, but it brought back the color and at least a false sensation of renewed strength to the ill man. Abel rolled his eyes sideways. "Alex, what happened?"

"You gave out as we were loading, then you passed out. Abel, you consarned half-wit, you scairt the hell out of me. And I'm going to tell you, you pig-headed old billy goat, this is the last time you're goin' to come up here to make wood."

"No, Alex. I'll be all right an' next year — ."

Alex's neck swelled. "If you do," he retorted fiercely, "you do it without me . . . an' that means my horses. Abel, what in tarnation will it take to make you see the light? You come within an ace of dyin' right here, today. If it hadn't been for the lad there, you would have as sure as I'm settin' here."

"The lad?" He rolled his eyes in the opposite direction. "What did you do?" he asked the Indian boy.

"Put a hollow reed down your throat and

76

breathed hard for you because you couldn't breathe for yourself."

Abel continued to gaze at the youth through a long period of silence, then he struggled to sit up and reach for the bottle, but Alex firmly pushed him back. "Lie still. Foster, hand me that bottle will you? Abel, don't you do anythin' but swallow. You hear me? Now swallow."

Eventually Abel slept. Until then Alex, Foster, and Jumping Mouse sat close and watched him. After he was sleeping, Alex stiffly got upright, swung his arms, leaned left and right, and raised his old hat to run bent fingers through his coarse gray hair.

He looked at the Indian youth. He wagged his head and finally showed a lessening of the strain in his face. He smiled and turned toward Foster. "You wasn't here. He grabbed the chain when Abel passed out. If he hadn't, I couldn't have held that damned log by myself an' it would have rolled back real fast. Maybe him and me could have jumped clear, but Abel was unconscious. That log would have squashed him flatter'n a pancake."

Foster gazed at the boy. "What was that business about a reed?"

Alex explained, then raised the bottle for two more swallows of its gut-searing contents.

Foster did not gaze at the youth this time;

he just looked at Abel and wagged his head. "Wasn't his time, is all I got to say."

They were through for the day even though it was still early. They sat like three morose crows on a fence watching Abel sleep. He snored and coughed weakly, which brought all three of them straight up, but he then resumed normal breathing.

In the distance one of Alex's big horses whinnied. As Alex turned to squint out where the horses had been grazing, Foster said, "If they wasn't geldings, I'd swear one of them was horsing."

Alex turned fully around and swore. "Damn it, look out there. Wild horses."

He was correct, but the mustangs were not easily seen through the dust banner that rose in their wake. They were beginning to slack off from a hard run, the dust overtook them, making them appear almost wraith-like in the sunlight.

Alex started toward camp with long strides. Foster stood up and watched as he said, "If that horse hadn't bellowed, they'd have run on past." He was right. Some of the mustangs — there seemed to be about seven or eight, counting big colts — continued eastward, but one particular horse rammed down to halt with his head high. They heard him whistle up as far as the wood-making area. Foster said, "Stud-horse. Now there's going to be hell to pay. If he comes for Alex's horses, he's goin' to get shot."

Alex was already rummaging for his Winchester. When he finally found it, he straightened up, legs wide apart, squinting with his one good eye out where the wild stallion was still obscured by dust. The range was much too great for a carbine.

Alex's big horses were coming around, heads forward. They saw nothing but the stallion, not even the three or four mares who had stopped running when he had.

Foster said, "Stay with Abel," to Jumping Mouse, and went swiftly down in the direction of camp.

Alex was already walking southward. He was keeping the bulk of his bays between himself and the distant stallion. He was not a good shot and had no illusions about being able to hit the wild horse, unless he could get fairly close.

One of the bays made a little sashay in the direction of the stallion, stopped and flung up his head to whinny again. It could have been a challenge or it could have been a demonstration of curiosity, but to wild horses that kind of a maneuvre was a battle signal. The stallion bobbed his head several times and pawed until dust flew, then he cakewalked a little before lining out in the direction of the team animals. He halted once, proudly erect, head high, and made his challenging whistle again. It was a sound that carried a great distance. He had his tail arched.

He was not a large horse in comparison to the draft animals; he could have been at the most fifteen hands high, and because the feed was abundant and strong this early time of year, he was rounding out after a hard winter. Handsful of loose, dull hair hung from him, with new hair beneath showing a shiny, faintly coppery sheen. Later, when the grass was less washy and had more strength to it, he would come up to perhaps a thousand pounds. Right now he was about eight hundred and fifty pounds — all bone, muscle, sinew, and fighting horse.

The rough-looking old rumpsprung mares, dowdy from dropping colts every year since they were three-year-olds, watched from farther back. One of them looked over her shoulder westward, then came around with coon-footed springiness, bobbed her head and snorted. That brought the other mares around to stare in the same direction. The stallion paid no attention until the mares whirled in unison and ran, heads up, tails straight out, going eastward where the other members of the band had gone.

The stallion turned his head to watch their flight, then turned back to look at the draft horses, and faunched a little with indecision. Finally, as Alex sank slowly to one knee and raised the Winchester, the stallion whirled on sprung hind legs, front legs clear of the ground, and came down lining out eastward in a dead run. Alex fired. Wherever the bullet went, it clearly was nowhere near the running wild horse because he did not even change leads. But the explosion from behind startled his big horses; they swung clumsily and went lumbering in panic in the same direction the wild horses had taken.

Alex stood up briefly to watch, then swore so loudly Foster could hear him very clearly. Even Jumping Mouse, much farther away, heard him.

He was still standing out there glaring after his horses and red as a beet when two riders came down-country in a long lope, and passed into the dust-haze which was still hanging in the motionless air. As one of them raised his arm in a high salute, they began to separate and widen the distance between them as they closed swiftly on the big lumbering bays.

Alex turned and stood wide-legged as he watched. Foster leaned to fill a tin cup with coffee, then he also watched, but his interest was not in the bays. It was in the pair of centaurs coming up on the bays from each side. Foster smiled, sipped coffee, and as Alex turned back toward camp, Foster laughed to himself. Alex walked up in a sweat, leaned his Winchester aside and held out his hand as Foster handed him a cup of coffee.

"Good thing the Templetons come along, Alex, or that stallion would have ambushed your team an' skinned 'em alive. . . . Alex?"

"What!" he answered grumpily.

"Alex?"

"Now what?"

"Ever since we been comin' up here Abel's been after you to hobble your horses when you turn them loose. Now maybe you'll do it."

Alex emptied the cup, tossed it aside, and watched as the Templetons came around on his big horses, hazed them down to a trot, then began driving them back. He was a hardheaded man, and even if he hadn't been, he would not have enjoyed having to eat crow, but quite possibly getting his horses back uninjured had something to do with his reply to Foster.

"All right, I'll hobble them," he growled, went looking for the hobbles and when he had them, walked down where the Templetons were coming up with the bays.

Bart Templeton was on the ground talking

soothingly to the draft animals when Alex got there. Bart's wife was still in the saddle, not entirely because she wanted to be ready if the big horses tried to whirl and run again, but also because she had caught sight of someone on the ground up beyond the camp, and it looked like an injured man to her.

Bart grinned as Alex went up to his nearest bay horse, sank to one knee, and disgustedly buckled on the hobbles. "We were on the trail," he said to the one-eyed man. "It never crossed my mind your horses would be loose out there."

"Well, they won't be loose no more," stated Alex, going over to hobble the other bay horse. As he arose he said, "You was after that band?"

"Not exactly. We'd finished fixin' up one of the salt traps when they came through the trees. They weren't any more surprised than we were. When they busted around and ran for it, we decided to get a look at them."

Nan Templeton interrupted. "Is someone injured? Up there where the wagon is standing, on the ground half in shade. Is that someone on the ground?"

Alex mopped sweat as he replied. "Yes'm. It's Abel Morrison. We was chain-falling a log up atop the load an' his heart gave out. He's better now, but I'll tell you, for a while there he had me scairt half to death. Got blue as a rock of turquoise, passed out. That In'ian boy saved his bacon. Stuck a hollow reed down his gullet and blew into it. I never even heard of such a thing before."

Nan's large, liquid dark eyes went to Alex Smith's face. "Heart trouble? Has he ever fainted like that before?"

"No ma'am, not that I know of. But for a fact he's got heart trouble. Has had it for years."

She frowned slightly and looked up the slope again. "Then what in the world is he doing up here doing this kind of work?"

Alex looked from Nan to her husband as he said, "Don't ask me, ask him, the darned fool . . . You folks come on up an' we'll eat. I'm real obliged for you bringing back my horses. It won't happen again. I'll keep them hobbled."

Nan dismounted and with her husband led her horse behind Alex up to the camp. They cared for their animals, then thanked Foster for the cups of hot coffee he handed them. Nan took her cup with her as she started up where Abel was sleeping. Up there she smiled at the youth and said, "Hello, Jumping Mouse."

"Hello, Missus Templeton. You people can call me Jim Moore — that was my name at the reservation school."

She accepted that. "How is he?" she asked, jutting her chin Indian-fashion toward the sleeping man on the ground.

"Sleeping now. I guess he is better. He fell down an' passed out when he was loading a log."

Nan knelt and looked closely at Abel. He was breathing deeply and rhythmically. She arose and smiled at the Indian. "Mister Smith said you saved his life."

His eyes darted away from her face. "He maybe would have been all right anyway."

She sipped coffee and regarded the Indian boy for a long moment, then went thoughtfully back to camp where her husband, Foster, and Alex were deep in a discussion of trapping wild horses, which only Bart had ever done with consistent success over the years. Alex and Foster, like a great many other men, had tried their hand at it at one time or another. They knew the several methods that were used, but neither of them had been successful enough to choose horse-trapping as a way to make a living.

Nan sat and listened, sipped her coffee, and when Foster eventually noisily rummaged in the grub box, she arose to help him prepare a meal. As they worked apart from Bart and Alex, she asked about the Indian boy. Foster told her what he knew. She was interested in what they intended to do about him when they left Wild Horse Mesa.

Foster glanced at Alex's back before lowering his voice as he replied. "Well, at first Alex was so mad about him takin' the horses he didn't care if the lad stayed up here and starved. But now — I've known Alex Smith a long time, ma'am. Now I got a hunch he'll take the lad with him when we head down out of here, maybe tomorrow."

"And the boy?"

Foster smiled. "He's a strange youngster, for a fact. For a couple of days he wouldn't talk, least of all to Alex. Now, him and Alex talk together. I think the boy's goin' to follow Alex around like a puppy."

Nan sat down with a dented, none-too-clean large old wash pan in her lap as she started peeling potatoes, and asked if Alex was married.

Foster shook his head. "No. Widower I expect."

"What does he do for a living?"

"Owns the gun shop down in Holtville."

Nan let the discussion end there and concentrated on peeling potatoes.

CHAPTER 7
ONE IDLE DAY

Bart Templeton listened as Alex told him they weren't going to put a cap log on the wagon; they had enough wood without it. He said he was not going to risk another accident. What he left unsaid was that he had a superstitious uneasiness about that log.

Bart said, "You're through up here then?"

Alex nodded. "Yep. We can head for home tomorrow."

"What about your partner up yonder?"

Alex flung the dregs from his coffee cup and put the cup aside. "We'll make him a soft bed atop the rig, where that cap log was supposed to go."

Bart looked pensive. "It might be better to wait a few days. He's a sick man. If you need more grub, we brought up quite a bit and you're welcome to some of it. Maybe in three, four days he'll be well enough to make it. Seems to me from what I've heard, this kind of heart trouble is serious."

Alex grew thoughtful. "He's sick all right. Dang near died."

There was a slight commotion out where the hobbled big horses were. He glanced down there. His big horses were looking southward, the direction the wild horses had taken. Alex muttered under his breath. "They're comin' back."

Bart shook his head. "I doubt it. Not as wary as that bunch was. Maybe tomorrow but not this soon."

Alex continued to watch his horses. When they eventually dropped their heads to crop grass, he settled forward and picked up the conversation where it had stopped. "We could wait a few days, an' thanks but we got more than enough grub." The big horses squared around again, doing as they had done before, standing like statues looking westward, ears up and bodies tense. "It's something," Alex muttered and pushed up to his feet.

Bart walked down away from the trees with him. When they were far enough southward to have an unobstructed westerward view, there was nothing to be seen. Alex puckered his good eye. "Maybe they picked up a scent — bear, maybe."

Bart raised an arm. "Horsemen. Up closer to the timber. Watch up there near that leaning big old snag."

Alex tipped down his hat and watched. "Sure enough," he said, sounding puzzled. "Looks like four of 'em. I wonder who they are an' what they're doin' up here."

The distant riders reined northward up through the timber and were lost to sight. Alex shrugged them off. "At least it wasn't them damned wild horses again," he said, and led the way back where Foster and Nan had put together a meal. She took two tin plates of food up where Abel and the Indian boy were sitting comfortably, talking. Abel would have arisen when she came along, but she scowled at him. "Sit there," she said, kneeling and handing each of them a plate. She smiled at Abel. "How do you feel?"

He made a rueful grin. "About like someone who's been pulled through a knothole. Jim was telling me about the ruckus over Alex's horses runnin' off." His smile faded. "I've told him at least fifty times to hobble them. They are his pets, like children to him. If the angel Gabriel come along with his golden trumpet and told Alex to hobble those horses, he wouldn't do it."

Nan smiled. "They're hobbled now."

Able glanced southward, out where the big horses were grazing, then back at the beautiful woman. "About time," he growled.

She watched them eat and offered to go

back for coffee, but Abel shook his head at her. "No. Jim here'll do it, won't you?"

The youth arose, smiled, and walked down the slope. The moment he was gone, Nan brought up the subject of what was to become of him. Abel spoke between mouthfuls. "We'll take him down out of here with us. I got the harness works in Holtville. I can teach him a trade. Maybe he could go to school, too, although he's already had some schooling."

Nan said, "How old do you suppose he is?"

"Sixteen. He told me that."

"Mister Morrison, have you talked to him about going to town?"

"No. We've talked about everything else, though: his folks, life on the reservation. His troubles."

"I wonder," Nan said thoughtfully, "if he's ever lived in a town."

"I'd guess he hasn't, ma'am."

"Mister Morrison, do you suppose he might be happier out in the country away from people. He's been a blanket Indian."

Abel lowered the plate and studied her face. "You got something in mind, ma'am?"

"Do you know my father, John Holbrook?"

"Yes'am."

"His ranch adjoins our place — my husband's homestead. There are miles of deeded land, open country, not many people."

"You want the boy?"

"Mister Morrison, we could give him a good home, and in time we could bring him into ranch life, give him a basic education along with some values he's going to need someday, when he's older."

"Does your husband like the idea, ma'am?"

Nan looked uncertain for the first time since the discussion had started. "I haven't mentioned it to him yet. First, I wanted to know what you and Mister Smith thought of the idea."

Abel raised the plate and resumed eating. Behind the beautiful woman down the slope, the youth was approaching with a tin cup in each hand. Abel smiled. "I can't answer for Alex, but for myself — I think you got a real good idea. I could ride out now an' then?"

"You'd always be welcome."

"Well now, Miz' Templeton, before you bring this up with Alex, let me sound him out. He can be pretty stubborn at times, an' he's taken a shine to the boy."

She returned to the camp after the youth arrived. Down there, her husband, Alex, and Foster had reached an agreement. Because it would be unwise to move Abel for a few days and their work up on Wild Horse Mesa was finished, they would go over to the Templeton camp and help Bart catch some wild

91

horses. It was only a couple of miles; they could come back every day and see how Abel was making out.

Bart seemed pleased. Foster and Alex liked the idea. It would take up their time until Abel was well enough to travel. The three men had a drink on it. Nan asked what they would do with the Indian boy. Alex did not even hesitate. "Take him along. He's right handy."

Later, when Foster and Alex went up to explain the plan to Abel, Nan Templeton sat down beside her husband and smiled. He said, "It'll help. Two more sets of hands can make the work of patching the trap a lot easier."

She continued to smile. "Three sets of hands. Jim Moore, too." At his blank look she explained. "Jim Moore is the Indian's name." His expression brightened. "All right. I thought his name was Jumping Mouse."

"He told me it is also Jim Moore. We should get back now, before a bear scents up our supplies."

He went for their horses, and Nan trudged up the slope and told the older men they were going to leave. She thanked them for the meal and the company. They leaned in long silence watching her walk away. Eventually Foster said, "That's a lucky horsebreaker." Abel and

Alex solemnly nodded. Jim Moore walked over to stand beside the loaded wagon looking at it. When Alex joined him, the youth said, "We could have got Mister Templeton to help us chain that log up on top."

Alex fidgeted. "Yeah, we could have; only we don't really need that log. We got more'n enough firewood as it is. You know anything about catchin' wild horses, Jim?"

The youth turned. "No. My father went out with the others sometimes. They'd catch some. I never went along."

Alex nodded his head. "Then I expect you're goin' to learn how it's done. We're goin' to help Mister Templeton catch some." At Jim's questioning look Alex said, "Can't move Abel for a few days. It might put a strain on his heart, and he'd not likely survive another one of those failings so soon after the other one. We'll come over every day and look after him."

Jim accepted that. He and Alex started down to the camp to do the chores. On the way the boy asked Alex again if Nan Templeton was part Indian, and as before Alex shook his head because he did not know whether she was or not. Then he said, "Ask her, if it means that much to you. You don't feel easy around folks that ain't Indian; is that it?"

Jim's answer was short. "No, that's not it.

People are people. My mother told me that."

They put things together, so they could be loaded onto the big horses and taken up to the Templeton's horse camp. Most of the things they did not pack they would leave behind for Abel. The day was drawing to a close by the time they were finished.

Foster came down to stir up the fire and start a meal, and this time Alex pitched in to help. The three of them got along in an easy sort of way. The Indian youth seemed to have accepted the older men, and they had certainly accepted him.

When the food was ready and Jim was about to volunteer to take some up to Abel, Foster restrained him with a hand on the arm, a scowl, and a wag of his head.

Alex trudged up there with the plate and cup of hot coffee. Abel was chewing when his friend arrived. Alex squinted his eye. "Maybe chewin' isn't good for folks with bad hearts," he said.

Abel spat out his cud, not because of what Alex had said but because he was hungry and Alex was kneeling to hand him the plate and cup. He said, "A lot of things aren't good for folks with bad hearts or with good ones. Alex, when my time comes nothing can prevent it for even one minute, an' until it comes nothin' is goin' to kill me."

As Abel raised the plate and began to eat, he watched Alex get comfortable, then between mouthfuls he said, "About Jim."

"What about him? He's pullin' his weight."

"It's not that, Alex. If we take him to Holtville with us. Neither one of us is set up to raise a boy. He'd have to sleep on the floor at my shop or over at your place. And he's not a town In'ian."

Alex replied fervently. "Thank gawd for that."

Abel ate a while in silence marshaling arguments, then he put the plate aside. "We owe him, Alex. Me especially for savin' my bacon. He's a good boy, In'ian or not."

"I agree, Abel; I've known you a long time. When you get to talkin' like this you're up to something. What is it this time?"

But Abel was not going to be rushed. He launched into another spate of oratory. "Blanket In'ians are used to open country, the wind in their faces, game to hunt, mountains to — "

"Abel, you missed your calling. Instead of patchin' harness an' saddles you should have taken to writin' poetry. Will you get to the damned point!"

Abel turned his head. "None of the three of us got any business tryin' to raise a child, not even a half grown one, and you know it."

Alex squirmed to get more comfortable on the fir needles. His exasperation was apparent in his expression, but he said nothing; he just made elaborate gestures indicating that he was getting comfortable because he knew he was in for a long session. None of this was lost on Abel. He emptied the tin cup then said, "Miz' Templeton could give him a decent home, in big open country, an' they could teach him a trade and all."

"Did she say this?"

"Yes."

"She really wants him, Abel?"

"Yes."

"Her husband, too?"

"Well, she ain't brought it up with him yet. But Alex, she is a woman not one man in a million could say no to."

Alex sat for a long time in slouched thought. Daylight was fading before he spoke again. "I was kind of thinkin' of takin' him on myself. Make a lean-to room on the back of the shop and all."

Abel understood. The big horses were fine, but they were still horses. Jim Moore was a person. A lonely man could use something like big horses for a substitute only until the real thing came along. Abel leaned and rapped his friend on the arm. "We could ride out. Miz' Templeton said we'd be welcome any

96

time. Alex, be honest about it. They got a lot more to offer him than we have, an' what's important is how he's goin' to make out in the future."

Alex arose and brushed himself off. "Now you're beginning to sound like a preacher," he muttered and put a squinty look upon Abel. "What does the boy say?"

Able had no answer. He had mentioned none of this to him, and he doubted that Nan Templeton had. Alex's squint tightened. "You haven't told him, have you?"

"No. I haven't an' I don't think she did."

"Well now, Abel, you're all fired up about what's fair and all — wouldn't you say the first thing would be to leave it up to the lad?"

Abel nodded half-heartedly because he knew how sly old Alex could be. "All right, but neither one of us will mention it to him."

"Then how in hell is he going to find out?"

"Let Miz' Templeton tell him. That's fair and proper."

Alex fished for his makings and rolled a cigarette which he lit by racing a sulphur match across the seat of his britches while one leg was hoisted in the air. He inhaled, exhaled, looked down where the Indian boy and Foster Bullard were sitting beside a built-up evening fire, and trickled more smoke. He had been thinking some very private thoughts since the youth had saved Abel's life and might even have saved Alex's, too, by refusing to abandon the chain-fall and run for it. He raised his face to the dusky sky where light-splinters were beginning to feebly glow.

Abel interrupted his sombre thoughts. "Help me up. I'll go down near the fire and roll into my blankets."

Alex's head came down and around. "You stay just like you are. I'll fetch your bedroll to you. And some whisky."

"I could stand up if you'd lend me a hand."

"Abel, you confounded idiot," Alex exclaimed in exasperation. "You never learn do you? Four hours back you was standin' with one boot in the grave an' the other foot on a banana peel. You're a sick man. You got to favor your bum heart like I got to watch out for my one good eye. Now you just set there."

Abel sat there as his friend went back down in the direction of camp. He smiled in the gloom as he said, "Maybe I'm an idiot but, by gawd, I know enough to hobble horses. And you just give the best argument why neither one of us had ought to take over Jim Moore. You can't see worth a damn an' one of these days I'm not goin' to wake up in the morning."

CHAPTER 8
HOBBLES

The Templeton camp was farther up in the timber high enough so that by climbing atop a scabrous old prehistoric rock three times as tall as a man on horseback, it was possible to look down upon about half of the mesa and a short distance farther westward upon the final stand of big trees where the horse trap was located.

By the time everyone got settled in, it occurred to Alex that his bay horses could not thrive in the forest. What bothered him was the long hike back down to the grassy plateau where he would have to take them.

Bart was sitting at the evening fire when he offered a solution of sorts. He said, "Nothing's spoiled the grass in the corrals very much. The feed's tall and strong in there. On the hike up here, you saw that the pole partition between the two corrals has rotted." He held out his cup for Nan to refill it before continuing. "Tomorrow we can snake down some green fir poles and fix that bad section, then we can put your big horses in the far corral."

Alex pulled on his cigarette while considering this suggestion. "Those horses can eat all the grass in there in one day."

Bart nodded. "Maybe after one day we can turn them loose outside the corrals."

Alex and Foster listened to the horsebreaker while Jim Moore and Bart's wife stowed the food and kicked the addtional bedrolls where they should go. They talked quietly to one another, ignoring the men at the fire.

Bart said, "Alex, we put two sacks of rock salt in the salt log you saw in the first corral."

Alex nodded. He had indeed seen the salt log with the mound of big white crystals in it. "That should bring 'em," he said, meaning wild horses.

"It should," agreed the horsebreaker. "And the smell of your horses ought to do the rest, make them willin' to come right on in."

Foster began to smile as understanding arrived. Alex, though, while not exactly averse to having his team animals used as bait, had reservations about the log partition they would build tomorrow being stout enough to prevent some orry-eyed wild stallion from getting at his bays. He said, "We better get an early start and snake down some pretty big logs."

Bart agreed. "Yeah."

With that topic taken care of, Foster asked why Bart bothered with wild horses at all, when he was known to have a fair-sized domestic herd of his own.

"It's real simple," Templeton stated. "I got a remount stud, Big Ben, he minds our mares very well. But sometimes he takes a crazy notion and comes up here to try an' steal some wild mares. Well, about ten days ago a wild stallion from up here reversed the process. He came down, fought Big Ben to a standstill, and herded about six of my open mares back up here. Nan and I were over at her pa's place and didn't even know the mares were gone for maybe three days after they were driven up here."

Foster grinned as he said, "So now you want your mares back."

Bart laughed. "With interest. I don't want the stud. I've got one horse that ran with mares up here. I don't need another one. I want my mares back and a few of the wild ones, too."

That made sense to the older men. Later, when they walked apart in search of their bedrolls, Foster was thinking of the difficulty men had who trapped wild horses; catching them was just about the easiest part. Getting a rope on them, then breaking them to lead or to drive were the hard parts. As he unrolled the bedroll, he looked over where Alex was sitting down tugging off his boots and said, "You reckon he rope-yokes them?"

Alex did not think so. "I wouldn't. Not an' try to drive them down that pair of ruts we came up here on. If one fell off it would take the other one with it, an' wild horses act crazy once they're caught."

Foster got into his blankets, settled low, then abruptly sat up to place his Winchester and Colt no more than ten inches from his ground-cloth. Alex saw him do this and grunted. "That's not goin' to happen twice the same week."

"Yeah? How do you know? This is bear country if I ever saw any."

They rolled their backs to one another and were momentarily quiet. Then it was Alex's turn to struggle around and sit up looking around. "Where's Jim?"

Foster took one arm from beneath the blankets and without speaking or raising his head, gestured in the direction of the dying fire, over where the Templetons had their bedrolls. Jim Moore was wrapped in someone's extra blanket already asleep next to the stone ring.

Alex considered that arrangement for a moment, then squirreled around to get beneath the blankets again as he said, "D'you know Miz' Templeton wants to keep the lad; raise him on the ranch an' teach him the cattle business and all?"

Foster knew. "Yes."

"An' I suppose you agree with Abel that it's a good idea."

Foster did not know anything about Abel thinking it was a good idea. *He* thought it was, though. "I think she's right. An' I think he might need a female to help guide him along. She's got a good, level head on her, Alex."

For a while Alex lay flat out looking up at the dark vault of the curved universe with his one eye. He did not say anything; he simply heaved up onto his side and composed himself for sleep.

Sometime in the night the big horses got restless, so Bart went out to them. Alex slept on. When Bart returned, his wife was waiting. He shook his head at her. "Nothing that I could see or hear. A scent I guess."

They settled in and did not awaken until the cold hour before sunrise. Jim was already pushing dry twigs into the coals and blowing on them. He had gone off to gather an arm-load of kindling before any of the others were awake.

Nan had disappeared up through the trees

wrapped in a blanket and did not reappear until her husband and the Indian boy had coffee boiling and meat frying. Alex and Foster came over after making themselves presentable. Breakfast was not a very noisy time. Afterward, the men picked up tools and went into the timber to select poles for the corral. It required the entire day, right up until the sun was setting, to cut, limb, and snake the logs down there, then to lever them into position and make them fit tightly between two uprights at one end, another pair at the opposite end, and a final pair in the middle. They had to make a gate where there had never been one, but on the outside, along the south side, not in the massive, high and very strong inner partition, because they did not want anything an enraged wild stallion might be able to batter down.

The last thing they did before walking wearily all the way up to the camp where Nan was preparing supper was put Alex's two bay horses in the partitioned-off corral.

Tired, the men said little at supper. There was no need for conversation anyway; each of them was speculating about the same thing: would the wild horses return tonight, and if so, would they be enticed into the salt-corral by the smell of Alex's horses? The clear answer was that if the horses did not appear tonight, they might do so tomorrow or the following night. They had become dependent on that salt log.

Later, before bedding-down time, Nan Templeton managed to maneuvre Alex away from the others, and after her first words he knew exactly why she had done this. She said, "Jim takes hold, doesn't he?" And before Alex replied, she added a little more. "It's as though he's been searching for a place to fit in, isn't it?"

"I expect he has been, ma'am. Being alone is bad enough for an adult, for someone his age, suddenly orphaned and movin' God-knows-where, it's a hard time."

"Mister Smith — "

"Alex, ma'am. Mister Smith was my pa an' he died a long time ago." Having got that settled between them, Alex tried to answer the concern he read on her face. "You're worryin' about the boy. He'll be all right. He's tough an' savvy and In'ians just naturally adapt, like coyotes or wild dogs."

She searched his face for the signs of denigration his remark had implied. All she saw was a lined, permanently roughened and darkened skin, and an expression of absolute candor. He had used those similies because he thought they fit, obviously unaware of their disparaging connotation.

"Alex . . . do you suppose living on a horse ranch, with freedom and substitute parents who care, would help him?"

"No doubt about it at all," he told her and waited for whatever came next.

"I talked to my husband about Jim."

"About takin' him home with you?"

"Yes. He — was surprised at first."

"I bet he was," Alex said dryly.

"But he likes the idea. He's a kindly man, Alex. He has more patience than most horse-breakers have."

"Ma'am, I already heard about this from Foster. I got to admit that I'd sort of figured on adopting Jim myself. But, like Foster said, I don't really have a place for him, and maybe comin' to live in town after bein' a reservation In'ian, he wouldn't be happy. . . But the lad earned our likin' up here, and he sure earned our respect for some of the things he did, so if you folks take him home with you, Abel, Foster, and I'd like to know we'd be welcome to come out now an' then to visit him."

As she studied the hard, lined old face, she found the faint signs of disappointment. Impulsively, she stepped ahead, kissed Alex on his beard-stubbled cheek, then stepped back and smiled at him. "You would be welcome any time, even if it weren't for Jim." She paused. "He'll need uncles. Alex, I don't think he could have three better ones."

Alex hadn't moved or blinked since that kiss. She had caught him totally off-guard. He had time to recover while she was speaking, so when she finished he said, "Who is goin' to ask the boy, ma'am? It's really up to him."

Her liquid-soft, very dark eyes were on his face as she said, "Would you do it? He respects you very much."

Alex grinned. "He should. He's the first horse thief I ever come onto that I didn't go after tooth and fang. Yes'm, I'll talk to him."

He watched her walk back through the soft night toward the fire, which was down to nubbins now. Then he heaved a big sigh and went over to his bedroll.

For a confounded fact Fate was a meddling, devious, sly-acting son of a bitch if there ever was one. A man came up to an isolated, uninhabited big plateau for the simplest of all reasons, to cut firewood, and lo and behold everything under the sun that could infuriate him — scare the hell out of him — annoy and upset him — then make his heart ache because he had found, and lost, something that would have filled his remaining years with interest — happened.

A man went to these far places for a little serenity. Hell, he might as well have stayed in town! In fact he'd have been better off if he had stayed in town. He sat down on the bedroll heavily and slumped a little. He was tired, he was also sad when Foster came along showing ivory teeth by starlight. Alex glanced up at him disapprovingly, "What the hell are you so happy about?"

"That's my natural disposition. It just naturally makes me feel good to be with people I like."

Alex looked down again. He wanted to snarl at someone but after Foster's last remark he couldn't do it. He kicked out of his boots, shed his hat, emptied the contents of his pockets into the hat, and pawed around to get beneath the blankets. As a sort of detached afterthought he said, "You reckon those wild horses will come tonight?"

Foster was getting ready to roll in. "If that wily stud horse doesn't smell us up here."

"We're too far for that," Alex said drowsily.

Foster chuckled. "I wouldn't be too sure of that. This afternoon down yonder, sweatin' like a mule, I got a whiff of a billy goat, and when I turned around lookin' for him, hell, it was me." Foster laughed at his joke, and Alex managed to faint smile.

Sleep came swiftly for everyone. The fire died away to hidden coals, a foraging owl came sailing low against the scent of two-legged things, and only at the last moment saw where he was. With powerful, frantic beats of his wings, he fought for enough altitude to make it down in the direction of the open country.

Tonight there was a late, sickle moon the color of old brass, its path through the myriad stars established long ago.

Once, a wolf sat back and sounded at a great distance. No one stirred among the bedrolls. Another time there was a faintly abrasive sign from lower down, out where the timber yielded to flat country and level land. That too went unheeded by the bedroll occupants.

Cold came stealthily, arriving late toward the darkness of very early morning. It increased as it settled low to the earth. Accompanying it was a depth of endless silence. This period lasted until a flung back streak of diluted red appeared all along the uneven and very distant horizon. Shortly after this, an occasional drowsy bird made a croaking call from the treetops.

Jim came out of his blanket to hunker at the fire ring poking for coals, and when he found them he placed thin, very dry twigs in a careful fretwork, then bent over and blew, continued to blow until a pencil-sized blue flame arrived.

He pulled on his worn-out old boots, swung

his arms against the cold, and went back up through the trees for an armload of more dry kindling. Behind him Nan turned and reached across to the adjoining bedroll to roughen the hair of her husband until he awakened and tried to catch her fingers. He was not fast enough.

The fire was burning well when they sat up and looked down there. It did not disturb them that there was no sign of Jim. There hadn't been any sign of him the day before when he'd stirred up the fire either, until he returned from the forest with an armload of dry sticks.

Bart glanced at his wife. "Did you hear horses last night?"

She hadn't. "No. Did you?"

He was reaching for his boots when he replied. "I didn't hear anything last night. The world could have come to an end, and I wouldn't have known about it until this morning."

She eyed him fondly. "You work too hard."

He smiled at her, then leaned to pull swollen feet into cold boots. "People die from not working enough; I never heard of anyone dyin' from doing his share."

"Yes, you did. Abel Morrison. He almost died."

He stood up with his hat on the back of his

head to watch the Indian youth approaching from the forest. He was carrying something, but it wasn't kindling wood. "We'd better ride over and see how Abel's doing today . . . What's Jim carrying?"

She sat up, holding the blanket to her body with both hands. For five seconds she did not speak, then she said, "Hobbles," with a sudden rush of breath.

Bart went quickly to meet the boy. Jim did not say a word, he simply held up four sets of Mormon hobbles and looked steadily at Bart, who reached, took the hobbles, and turned with them toward the firelight. Each set had been unbuckled. It was not unheard of for hobbled horses to get free, particularly if they grazed through low, spiny bushes that could catch the tongue of leather and hold it until the buckle was released. But there was no underbrush where the Templeton animals had been left, and it was unbelievable that the same accident could occur to four horses at the same time.

Bart let the hobbles hang at his side as he faced the youth. Jim pointed. "They're gone. All four of them."

Bart gazed up in the direction of the small glade where he had left the animals. His mind was perfectly clear. He handed back the hobbles and started up past the trees. Jim hesitated, then followed. The fire could wait, or someone else could stoke it.

There was no dawnlight in the little clearing even though feeble newday light was appearing elsewhere. The surrounding big trees kept it out.

When Bart stopped, the only thing he saw was that the glade was empty. Jim stood beside him for a moment, then walked out and around, making a circuit of the glade. He stopped twice, the first time for only a moment, but the second time, when he was nearly opposite Bart Templeton, he leaned, then finally sank to one knee, and this time when he raised his head Bart was already walking toward him.

The tracks were identifiable as the marks left by shod horses; four of them walking in a row. It was impossible to make out much more until the dawn widened the scope of its penetration.

There was no grass beyond the glade, just layers of spongy fir needles. Jim paralleled the tracks, which were faint, but not as faint as they would have been if there hadn't been dew during the night. Bart moved with the youth, but upon the opposite side of the tracks, and it was Bart who stopped abruptly, dropped to both knees and leaned close as he traced out a boot-track with one finger.

Jim continued to scout for signs. Eventually he too found boot tracks, and by the time Bart caught up, he had found something else: a place among the trees where a number of men had been on the ground with horses. They must have been there quite a while, judging from the droppings of their animals.

Jim picked up something moist and sticky, held it up on his palm for Bart to sniff, then dropped the sticky object as Bart said, "Cud of chewing tobacco. Let's get back, Jim. We've been raided by horse thieves."

The Indian was almost apologetic as they started back. "I didn't hear anything last night."

Bart looked down and roughly slapped Jim on the shoulder. "Neither did I. Horsethieves like this bunch don't make noise. Not even a little noise. Yesterday when Alex's horses were acting skittish, he and I walked down there; west of us riding up close to the timber, we saw four horsemen."

Jim looked up. "Them?"

"Wouldn't surprise me none," Bart said, and widened his stride at the sound of activity down at the camp.

Jim had to almost trot to keep up. Normally he had a big appetite. The older men had marvelled at the amount of food he could put away. This morning as he followed Bart down into camp, he had no appetite at all.

CHAPTER 9
WILD HORSE MESA

What Bart had to relate did not really surprise anyone — not after Nan explained her husband's absence by mentioning the empty hobbles. Alex wasn't there to drink hot coffee with them, and he did not appear, red in the face from exertion, until they were toying with their food. He stopped a hundred or so feet from them and bellowed. "They're gone! My horses are gone!" He panted the rest of the way to the stone ring and sank to the ground. "We tied that gate closed from the outside. There's not a horse alive with a neck long enough to reach over and down that far from the inside and worry that knot loose."

Bart nodded, but he took the loss of Alex's horses as a serious blow because now they were on foot. Men on foot rarely overtook men on horseback, expecially if the men on horseback knew the men on foot would be hunting for them with murder in their hearts.

Alex raised his bloodshot eye to Bart. "Sure as I'm setting here it was those riders we saw yesterday. Four of 'em. Remember?"

Bart remembered. He was past shock and was already thinking ahead. The dilemma was they were on foot in a country where distances were so vast that a walking man might just as well not be moving at all.

Jim slipped away, climbed that scabrous old rock northwest of camp, and for a long time lay belly down atop it, like a lizard. When he eventually came back to camp he said, "I saw them," and jutted his chin southward. "A long distance. Four riders driving four small horses and two big horses."

Nan had a flicker of hope. "Southward? They will cross our range and my father's range. Maybe my father's riders will see them. If they do, they'll know the Templeton brand."

None of them mentioned what occurred to each of them. Horse thieves driving branded horses would not go anywhere near a set of ranch buildings, neither would they risk being seen by riders if they saw the riders first. Perhaps luck would intervene, but that was not anything a man wanted to hang his hopes on.

Bart drained his coffee cup and put it aside as he arose. He looked a long time at the Indian's cracked, broken old worn-down boots before he said, "You up to a little dog-trotting?"

Jim understood at once, which was more than the others did. He stood up, picked up three soggy hoecakes, dropped them into a ragged pocket, and nodded his head.

Nan stared incredulously at her husband, watching him shed his shell belt and shove the naked six-gun into the back of his waistband, reset his hat and grin wolfishly at the boy. She said, "The ranch is almost thirty miles, Bart."

He turned, leaned to roughly kiss her, and said, "We don't have to go that far. You're forgetting about the Wiltons, Nan." He turned toward Alex and Foster, whose faces were rigidly expressionless. "Might be a good idea if you went over to see how Abel's getting along. Don't worry. We'll get back as soon as we can . . . Jim?"

The seated people watched Bart and the lean Indian boy strike out downhill. The old men were silent, but Nan wasn't. "I'm afraid," she said candidly. "One man and a boy against four outlaws."

Foster turned from watching the departing figures to regard the woman. "What did he mean — you forgot about the Wiltons?"

"Last year some emigrants got stranded on the north range, up near the foothills about three miles east. Their baby was ill and the woman almost died birthing it. They couldn't

117

move on. My father gave them a hundred acres up there."

Foster's eyes widened. "How far from here?"

She had to guess. "Six, maybe eight miles."

Foster smiled as he glanced at Alex. "Well, now, that's better'n thirty miles to the ranch."

Alex nodded, then asked Nan a question. "Do those emigrants have saddle animals?"

"One," she replied, still standing and facing southward, watching her husband and the youth called Jim Moore break clear of the timber and strike out across the wide plateau. "One saddle animal and two team horses."

She turned away from the seated men and became busy putting the camp in order, her head averted most of the time. They arose and solemnly pitched in to help, and later, when she left them to walk back toward the scabrous rock to climb it for her last sighting of the tiny figures out across the mesa, Alex and Foster put some food in a cloth and struck out through the timber in the direction of their old camp.

The hopes they had abandoned upon discovery that all the horses had been taken, had been resurrected with the revelation that Bart would not have to go all the way down to the Holbrook place. They discussed the possible results of this new condition, and even Alex

118

was cheered by it. Two men, a man and a boy who were good physical specimens, could probably reach the emigrant camp a little past noon. If Bart borrowed the settler's saddle horse, he could cover the balance of the distance to the Holbrook yard in good time, and after that he could take up the pursuit on a fresh horse, with John Holbrook's riders to back him up.

As he and Foster approached their old camp, Alex was enormously relieved that he would probably get his horses back. Before, he had almost abandoned hope.

Abel was over at the creek shaving with a straight razor, cold water, and lye soap. He had a steel mirror propped against a rock. When he heard them coming, he twisted with the razor poised, then went back to finish shaving as Foster arrived first, with Alex a few yards to the rear. Foster blurted the story, and Abel turned slowly to stare at him, holding the razor poised again.

Alex told Abel about the Wiltons, and Foster dropped on his belly at the creek to drink as Abel and Alex discussed Bart Templeton's prospects. At first Abel had been shocked; now he said, "Last night, real late, I thought I heard horses walkin' along up above in the timber. It didn't make sense. Wild horses wouldn't go up in there, especially at night. I guess I should have gone up to look around, but I didn't."

Foster was back on his feet, flinging off water as he said, "Most likely it's a danged good thing you didn't. Sure as hell they've had shot you . . . We brought you some grub."

Abel took the little bundle and led the way back to the shade of his bedroll area on the east side of the loaded wagon. It was ready to be pulled back down off the plateau, but there were no horses to pull it.

Abel sat down, looked at the food that had been rolled all together, and began eating. Occasionally he glanced at Alex, who was rolling a smoke, grim in the face and dourly silent.

Abel asked where Nan was. Alex trickled smoke as he replied. "Wanted to be alone."

Abel bobbed his head in understanding, then asked several questions about the Wiltons and their camp. All his friends could tell him was what Nan had told them, which was not very much: the distance to the camp was not excessive, and there was a saddle animal down there.

The thieves had stolen all their horses, which meant any pursuit would be on foot in a very isolated and uninhabited area. They were probably very satisfied with themselves, and they would have had a right to be if there had not been an emigrant camp where their victims could get help only a short distance from the mesa, down along the timbered foothills to the east.

Abel finished eating and drank from his canteen. He felt good; not strong and a little intimidated by his close brush with death, but well enough to think clearly.

He thought he would go back to the horse camp with his friends, but when he mentioned it Foster very quickly came down hard in opposition. So did Alex.

Abel did not argue. His friends split enough wood to keep him warm for several days, rested for another hour or so, then told him they would return the next day and departed. They trailed back through the timber by the same route they had used to get over there.

When they were gone, Abel picked lint off a plug of Mule Shoe, carved off a corner with his clasp knife, got the cud settled comfortably in his cheek, and sat back gazing off in the direction of the creek. He could walk over there; he wouldn't carry much, just his possible-bag which contained his soap, razor, and two extra plugs of tobacco, and his blankets. There did not have to be climbing, or at least very little, and he would rest often.

He would also catch hell when he walked out of the forest into their camp, but that did not bother him; in fact, he grinned in anticipation.

The sky was clear to the horizon. That obscure veil which had been up there a few days ago had not presaged rain after all. A slight, ground-hugging little breeze came to stir dust and sigh its way southward toward open country. It seemed to come from the north, but evidently it didn't because it carried with it the putrid aroma of a dead bear.

When he got back to town he would go see Doctor Mailer but he really did not believe he had to; a man was as good a monitor of his own physical workings as a medical man would be. Better, in fact.

Abel arose to move around a little. It had been borne in upon him last night while he was lying sleeplessly in his blankets that this would be his last visit to Wild Horse Mesa. It was a sobering and saddening thought, but among the many gruff remarks Alex Smith had made was one that Abel knew he could not dispute. He should not have come up here this time. What had happened to him was about as dire a warning as a man could get. The next time he exerted himself as he had the day before yesterday would be the last time.

He picked up the possible-bag, rolled the blankets, slung them over one shoulder, tied them at the bottom on the left side, and began picking his way without haste over the tracks of Foster and Alex. It was cool and fragrant in the timber, which was a blessing because out across the plateau where there was nothing to mitigate the late springtime sunshine. It was hot enough to make heat waves.

The third time he halted to ease down upon a punky old deadfall fir to rest, three striped chipmunks arrived to stand as tall as they could looking at him. One made a tiny barking sound, which Abel assumed was a warning to the others not to get too close. He laughed at the way they stood, tiny hands across their chests, looking straight up at him. Five inches tall and absolutely serious.

The laughter scattered the small creatures like autumn leave in a wind.

He resumed the hike, and knew he did not have much farther to go when he detected wood-smoke at a time when there was not a breath of air stirring. Eventually, he heard voices. One belonged to a woman. Through the trees slightly southward was the camp with people at the stone ring preparing supper.

He suddenly felt hungry. He probably had been all along, but it was the cooking-fire aroma and the sight of people starting to make a meal that made him conscious of hunger.

He strode down across that little glade

where the horses had been, where the Indian boy had found the hobbles lying in wet grass, and emerged upon the upper rim of the camping site where Foster saw him immediately and stopped feeding wood into the fire in astonishment.

Alex looked around. So did Nan, but she reacted differently from the men: she arose and walked forward smiling. She took his blanket roll and led the way back where Foster and Alex were making a point of working with pots and pans so they would not have to look up.

Nan got Abel a cup of coffee. He thanked her and with a twinkle in his eyes, gazed at his friends. Alex refused to look up, but Foster did. "Suppose," he said, "you'd had another of them seizures back yonder in the trees?"

"I didn't, Foster," replied Abel as he sat down beside Alex. "Good to see you again," he said, forcing Alex to finally face him.

Alex turned and said, "Yeah. An' you're damned lucky you're able to."

Nan watched and listened, and changed the subject by saying she thought that by now her husband and Jim Moore should have reached the Wiltons' camp. "On horseback they can get down to my father's yard by suppertime. With some luck."

Foster smiled broadly. "They'll overtake

those men. Maybe by tomorrow afternoon."

No one disputed this, but Nan's expression underwent a subtle change. Abel noticed this and soothingly said, "Well now, how many riders does your pa keep, ma'am?"

"Four full-time, Abel. During the busy season he sometimes hires on another two or three."

Abel spread his hands. "That sure evens up the odds, don't it?"

Nan smiled as she inclined her head. She understood perfectly what Abel was trying to do, and she appreciated it. She and Bart had been married one year. This was the first time she'd ever had occasion to really worry about him. She had worried a little at other times, as when he'd rig out a colt for its first ride, but she had seen him do that so many times now, understood so well how he used different tricks on different colts to bring them along without fighting him, that she could now watch him leave the yard astride a green horse and scarcely worry at all.

This was different. Altogether different.

She and Foster got the meal. Alex helped, but he had never been very handy at cooking. Abel was much handier, but he sipped coffee and watched. Two cooks were enough. Three cooks got in each other's way.

Alex asked in a lowered voice if Abel had

125

brought over one of the whiskey bottles. He hadn't, so Alex said he might walk back over yonder in the morning and get one.

It was a comfortable meal. There was no joking, and the conversation stayed well away of the topic uppermost in all their minds, but there were other things to talk about and Nan proved herself very good at putting the old men at ease and keeping them that way.

There was, they all knew perfectly well, not a thing any of them could do except wait. Worrying was inevitable but it was also useless. As Abel told Foster and Alex as they were rolling into their soogans well across the fire ring from where Nan would bed down, "What it boils down to is how long do we set up here like crows on a fence?"

Foster made a guess. "Two more days."

CHAPTER TEN
A DARK TRAIL

Emily Wilton was bathing her baby near the fire ring, too engrossed to hear anything but the child's little sounds, but her husband, who was near the tailgate of their old wagon patching harness, heard someone coming. He reached inside for his rifle as Bart and Jim emerged from the trees, red-faced from exertion and soaked with sweat. Emory Wilton froze for five seconds, then left the rifle and moved away from the tailgate as he said, "Mister Templeton!"

Bart smiled at the startled woman and then began to explain where he had come from, who Jim Moore was, and why they had arrived at the camp.

Emily wrapped her baby and held it close as she listened. Her gangling husband reacted quickly. "I'll go fetch the saddle animal. I'd better fetch one of the team horses, too." As he went for lead ropes he also said, "Yesterday Mister Holbrook's rangeboss came by." As he started down away from the camp, Bart and Jim followed along. The lanky emigrant eyed Jim with frank interest as they hiked out where three hobbled horses were grazing.

They were docile animals in good flesh because they had done nothing but drag a few firewood logs to the camp since last autumn. As Emory Wilton went up to rig them with lead ropes, he said he'd done a little riding this spring, when the weather permitted it, mostly to hunt for camp meat, so his horses weren't exactly green.

He knelt to remove the hobbles as Bart and Jim held the ropes. When he was finished and about to lead the horses back to camp to be rigged out, Bart fashioned two squaw bridles from the lead ropes, one on the saddle animal, the other on the draft horse, and told Wilton they would ride bareback.

The last thing Bart said before riding off was that he'd see the horses were returned. Wilton stood like a statue, looking bewildered as the pair of riders got their animals lined out southward. Then he turned and strolled back where his wife was dressing the baby on the tailgate. She looked up inquiringly. He said, "They left from down there riding bareback. Mister Templeton is sure in a hurry." The small woman nodded without commenting and went back to caring for her child.

The sun was slanting, faint shadows appeared, and although visibility was good, a gradual late-day haze began to form about the time Bart and Jim were a couple of miles from the emigrant camp.

Bart had been watching the pudding-footed big harness horse from the corner of his eye. Not all draft horses were broke to ride. In fact, while many were docile enough to submit to a man on their backs, they neither reined well nor responded to heel pressure. Wilton's big animal responded to Jim's heels, but it had to be squaw-reined, and even then the horse was hard to keep heading in a straight line. But at least he did not offer to buck or run.

Jim sat up there like a burr. He grinned when Jim looked over at him. The saddle animal had age on him, which mitigated the possibility that he might have bucked at being ridden by a stranger without a saddle or bridle. Once he understood what was required of him, he lined out in an easy lope and kept it up until the unusual exertion had him sucking air, and Bart hauled down to a walk. By then the saddle horse was also agreeable to being ridden without a saddle or bridle.

The distance from the Wilton camp to the Holbrook ranch yard was only slightly more than the distance Bart and the Indian had already covered on foot, but the day was waning. By the time they had the big trees, the rooftops, and the dusty yard in sight, visibility had been noticeably shortened.

They walked the horses for the last mile in order to have them arrive in the yard cooled out. That used up more time. As they walked in, the only noise came from the cook-house. The yard was empty. Bart went directly across to the main house, tied up, and headed for the porch. Jim hesitated, decided to remain with the horses and when an older man opened the door for Bart to enter, the Indian leaned on the tie-rack looking at the buildings, at the large network of pole working corrals behind and to one side of the horse barn, and the cook shack where there was noise.

John Holbrook gazed at his son-in-law, showing only a fraction of the surprise he had felt when he had opened the door. Bart started talking, and the older man went to a sideboard for two glasses of whiskey, handed one to Bart and took the other one with him as he went to the far end of the large room to take up a wide-legged stance with his back to a massive stone fireplace. When Bart had finished, John Holbrook said, "It'll be dark in another hour or so."

Bart sipped the whiskey, felt the fire spread

through his system, and nodded his head. "They were going due south," he said. "I hope they feel safe enough by now to make a camp for the night. What I'd like to do is ride south, too. Maybe they'll have a cooking fire, or maybe we'll be able to hear them."

Holbrook thought about this. "It'll be chancy in the dark, Bart."

"I know. But they've got a hell of a lead on us. If we can't nibble away at that, sure as hell they're going to make it out of the country. We'll be careful."

Holbrook's eyes widened a little. "We? You got Nan with you?"

"No. An Indian boy we found up in the mountains."

"I see. Well, suppose I send the cook and one man up to the mesa to help those folks, and you take my range boss and the other three men. Come morning you just might get a sighting. You got any idea who those horse thieves are?"

"None at all. There were four men riding west up close to the trees the day before the stock was stolen. They were too far off to see much about them. Just four men on horses."

"But you think it's them?"

Bart nodded, finished the whiskey and put the glass aside. "I think it's probably them, but I don't really care. I just want to catch up to whoever it is."

Holbrook turned to place his half-empty glass on the log mantle. "The men are having supper. I'll go down to the cook shack with you. Why not leave the Indian boy here? This isn't goin' to be something a person had ought to be involved with unless he's grown and armed and handy."

Bart turned toward the door as his father-in-law left the fireplace bound in the same direction. He was not sure he should leave Jim, and he was equally uncertain about taking him along, into a situation where there could very well be a gunfight.

As they walked down off the porch, John Holbrook halted to gaze at the emigrant's horses. He grunted, said nothing about the animals, and turned his attention upon the youth. "What's your name, lad?"

"Jim Moore."

"Well now, Jim, what's shaping up is likely to last all night and into tomorrow, an' you already been without sleep a long time, and from the looks of you, you been without groceries even longer. I think it would be best if you stayed here at the yard until Bart comes back."

Jim's thin face lifted, the dark eyes seeking Bart's face in the pewter gloom. Bart smiled slowly and shrugged wide shoulders. Jim looked back at John Holbrook. "I'd like to go along."

Holbrook threw up his hands. "All right. You come with us, and we'll fill a sugar sack with grub. Son, if you get any skinnier one of these days you're goin' to fall through a hole in the seat of your britches and hang yourself."

The riders had finished eating and were drifting out onto the cook shack porch to roll cigarettes. They all knew Bart Templeton, but he appeared different from the way they had usually seen him. They eyed the skinny Indian youth with equal interest. Charley Lord, the tough, rawboned Holbrook range boss smiled at Bart. "Find any horses up there?" he asked.

Bart smiled back. "Yeah, we saw a band, and we lost six of our own horses."

John Holbrook explained to the listening rangemen. The last thing he said was: "It's up to you. You been in the saddle all day, an' I've got a feeling this is goin' to be a long trail with trouble at the end of it."

Lanky Charley turned slowly, gazed at the four men behind him, turned back and said, "It'll take us maybe fifteen minutes to snake out fresh horses. Bart, you'n the lad better go inside and fill up while we're at it." He squinted through the gloom in the direction of the mainhouse tie-rack, then dryly said, "I expect you'll need another animal."

Bart said, "Two, Charley," and although Lord looked without much enthusiasm at Jim Moore, he said nothing, just turned to lead the way down off the porch in the direction of the horse barn.

John Holbrook led the way into the cook shack where a paunchy man with watery eyes and very thin brown hair was cleaning up. "Got a couple of starve-outs," the cowman said. The cook nodded to Bart, then considered Jim Moore with a coarse, expressionless face for a long moment. He said something guttural and waited. Jim's eyed widened in the lamplight. He answered in the same guttural language, and the cook laughed as he turned toward the stove. "Set," he said in English.

John Holbrook filled a cup with coffee for himself and stood near a window looking out as the cook piled two platters with food and put them on the long, littered table. Jim Moore followed the cook with his eyes. When the paunchy man turned and saw him doing this, he spoke again in that guttural language, and Jim Moore grinned at him without replying and started to eat.

As John Holbrook faced around, the cook said, "Shoshoni-Piute. It's been a while since

I've run across one. Years back I spent a trappin' season with 'em up north. They got a real fondness for white dogs. I never ate so much dog meat before nor since."

Someone had draped a lighted lantern in the barn runway. From its swaying illumination the men in the cook shack could look down there and watch men leading in horses to be rigged out. The cook was interested but said nothing as he worked at two big washpans with hot greasy water in them, until one of the riders went to the bunkhouse and returned carrying five saddlebooted carbines, then he straightened back, wiping both hands on his flour-sack apron and turning a quizzical gaze upon his employer.

Holbrook put his empty cup aside as he said, "Horse thieves, Henry. Raided Bart's horse camp up on the big mesa. Got his four animals and two big ones that belong to the gunsmith over in Holtville."

The cook continued drying his hands even after they were dry. "Got Alex Smith's big team?" He wagged his head. "Where is Alex?"

Bart answered. "Back up at the camp with Abel Morrison and Foster Bullard. They were making wood."

The paunchy man pursed his lips. "I'll tell you if I was the ones that stole Alex's horses, I

135

wouldn't even look back for five hunnert miles. He thinks more of them horses than he thinks of money."

Bart arose. Jim was still eating. The three older men watched owlishly as he ate, glanced around at one another, and rolled their eyes. But nothing was said.

Charley appeared in the doorway. "Ready, Bart. We fixed you'n your partner up with everything — couple of blankets behind the cantle and two Winchesters under the fenders." As he said this, the rangeboss looked from Jim to the plate in front of him, which had been swabbled clean with bread until it shone. He raised his eyes with a twinkle in the direction of the cook. "That's one you won't have to wash," he said and let the door close as he returned to the barn where the four men were waiting.

John Holbrook went after him. Later, when the men were ready to ride, there was one less rangeman. Down inside the barn, a disgruntled rider was stripping a horse with his back to the yard. He was the man Holbrook had almost forgotten to keep back to go up to Wild Horse Mesa in the morning with the cook.

Bart watched Jim climb astraddle and even up the reins. Charley also watched, and he smiled as he turned to toe into his own stirrup.

John Holbrook said, "Charley, you an' Bart be careful."

The lanky man nodded and turned to follow Bart out of the yard westward. A quarter of a mile they swung southward, but on an angling southwestern course. Bart had no idea how far out the horse thieves had passed, but he was sure it had not been anywhere within sight of the Holbrook buildings.

He knew the country they were riding over very well. He owned some of it, but farther west. Until they got over that far, they were riding on Holbrook range.

Charley drew ahead to ride beside Bart. He was wearing an old horsehide coat with red blanket lining. The coat had once been smoke-tanned pearl gray, now it was dark with age, scuffed from hard use, and stained from a hundred cooking fires.

It had at one time been adorned with fringes across the yoke and down the sleeves, but Charley had cut those fringes off fifteen years ago. Each winter since Bart Templeton had been in the country, he had encountered the rangeboss wearing that coat. As they rode along now, Bart gave the rangeboss most of the details of what had happened back up on the plateau. When he mentioned Abel Morrison's heart seizure, the rangeboss shook his head and said, "That's not the first one." At

Bart's look Charley said, "I know about two others. Once when I was standin' in his shop and he was pullin' hard to stretch a length of tug leather, he slipped and fell . . . swallowed his cud of tobacco. He flopped around like a fish out of water, liked to scairt me to death. I carried him to his bed in the back and ran for help."

"What happened?"

"He was sittin on the edge of the bed when I got back with that woman who did mid-wifin' around town before Doc Mailer came along. She snorted and stamped out to go home. Seems she'n Abel been through that once before. He wouldn't listen to her that time neither." As Charley finished, he showed a tough little rueful smile. "One of these days . . . "

They eased over into a lope. It was like hunting a needle in a haystack, which Bart had known it would be. Nor did he actually expect to find the outlaws. What he wanted to do was be far enough down-country by sunrise to possibly catch sight of them, or at least to be able to pick up their tracks and stay on them until they showed against the ground.

Jim and two of the riders farther back were getting along well. The rangemen teased the Indian, and they all laughed. Charley Lord watched this for a while then asked Bart about

Jim. The answer Charley got was slow arriving. "He's an orphan. Left some reservation up north because everyone was dying of some illness. Nan wants us to take him in."

The rangeboss eyed his companion askance. "How about you?"

Bart smiled. "I like the idea."

Nothing more was said on this topic. They hauled back down to a walk, held the horses at the gait for an hour, then booted them into a lope again. It was a good way to cover ground without wearing down saddlestock.

Charley wondered about how far ahead the outlaws were. Bart could not offer much of an estimate. His main hope was that wherever they were on the south range, since they had got no sleep last night because they had been too busy stalking horses to steal, and since by now they were a considerable distance from the mesa where they had stolen the horses, they might decide to bed down. If they did, Bart and the Holbrook riding crew were probably going to either find them or get close enough to see them by dawn.

Unless, of course, they had changed course during the night, in which case Bart and his companions would have wasted hours in the wrong direction. It was the kind of chance Bart had to take as long as he remained embarked upon his present course.

The stars brightened, and darkness lay in all directions. Occasionally they encountered cattle, which invariably lumbered up out of their beds and fled, and once they stopped because one of the riders held up his arm, saying he could smell wood smoke.

He was correct. They quartered for high ground, found none, and had to seek the source of that fragrance by fanning out and scouting in the direction where the smell was strongest.

An itinerant peddler and professional fix-it who traveled from town to town soldering broken kettles, sharpening scissors, and selling pots, pans, and medicines had a camp in a slight swale. His box-like light wagon with the shafts lying on the ground, was faintly silhouetted by a dwindling fire as the horsemen came up out of the night and halted. The peddler arose very slowly from his fire and stood as stiff as a ramrod. He was not a young man and was wearing a suit coat with a heavy woolen muffler around his throat and a battered old black derby hat. He had mittens from which the upper end of the fingers had been cut out.

He stood wide-eyed staring at the six riders five yards distant, shadowy and sinister in their silence as they studied his camp. One of the men, who looked tall and rangy even at that distance in the dark, said, "Good evening," in a deceptively mild, deep voice. "We're lookin' for some men driving six head of horses. Two of the horses are pretty close to a ton; real big animals."

The peddler, whose terror was genuine, was convinced as long as he lived that he had encountered the James gang along with the Younger boys. He raised a shaking arm to point. "Before sunset," he quavered. "There was four fellers went past headin' south drivin' some horses ahead of them. They was too far for me to make much out about them or the horses. There could have been two big horses. But I can tell you for a fact, gents, them horses was plumb worn down."

Charley thanked the peddler, and he could not resist a parting comment as he reined around. The man's terror was so palpable the horsemen could sense it yards away. Charley raised a gloved hand in parting salute as he called back. "My friend here, Wild Bill Hickok, says he's much obliged."

The peddler did not believe that for one minute. He had seen pictures of Bill Hickok. He wore his hair long. None of those men had long hair.

A mile farther along, with something now to give a degree of reassurance that they were not riding all over hell for nothing, the rangemen broke into laughter.

Bart slouched along in silence trying to come up with a reasonable evaluation. If the peddler had seen the horse thieves before sunset, and it was now getting along toward midnight, and if the outlaws were driving exhausted horses, which they probably were, then they would be unable to make good time and probably had not been able to make good time since midday.

His spirits rose a notch.

Charley was of the opinion that the outlaws would camp for the night. Bart hoped he was right, and suspected that indeed he might be. The previous night the outlaws had got no sleep. They had been in the saddle all day today, their stolen horses and probably their individual saddle horses as well, were wearing down. They could not hope to keep pushing tired horses indefinitely, but if they rested the animals overnight, they could make good time again tomorrow.

CHAPTER 11
THE LOW PLACE

Bart set the pace from here on, and it was slower than it had been. Everyone was alert. There was less hope now that they would see a campfire. Tired horse thieves were not likely to sit up until midnight, and campfires dwindled fast if they were not fed.

Occasionally he glanced back at Jim Moore. If the youth was tired, he was hiding it well. He had ridden straight up in the saddle from the time they had left the Holbrook yard. Bart watched the saddlebooted Winchester under the righthand *rosadero* of his saddle sway with the horse and thought that was probably the main reason the boy sat his saddle with pride. Bart had said nothing when he had seen the gun in place as they were mounting back at the yard, but he had not liked the idea.

The night was still, the only immediate sound that of shod horses, the whisper of leather over leather, an occasional man clearing his pipes, or mumbling to someone. Their pursuit had settled down into a slogging period of plain, everyday saddlebacking, something which was boring under most circumstances and certainly to the Holbrook riders who had already put in a full day of it.

Charley Lord speculated on the distance they had covered, and while he was doing this someone farther back made a hissing sound. It was one of those sounds that in itself was meaningless, except for its tone of urgency. Charley stopped speaking as he and Bart swiveled in their saddles.

Jim Moore was pointing with an upraised arm. "Smoke smell," he said.

They halted. The men tested the air, and for a while there was no scent, then a faint hint of a breeze came to them from the southwest. It had a barely discernible but identifiable smell of wood smoke to it.

Bart swung off. The other riders followed his example. Charley leaned on his saddle gazing out into the darkness. "Could be quite a distance," he opined, and no one disputed him.

Bart peered around the area where they had stopped. There were no trees that he could make out but there were patches of flourishing brush, mostly spiny chaparral with its tiny leaves and wiry branches.

There were rocks, mostly head-size and scattered, but occasionally there were much larger rocks clumped together in piles not much taller than a man on foot.

One of the riders asked if there was a ranch down here, buildings where stove or fireplace smoke could still be spreading into the air.

Bart shook his head. He did not know exactly where they were, but he had ridden this far south many times, over a wide area, and he had never seen buildings nor encountered anyone.

The rider said, "Then it's a campfire. Maybe it's them an' maybe it's pot-hunters, or emigrants."

Bart smiled at the rider. "Let's find out," he said and led his Holbrook horse toward a big buckbrush bush. They pulled out the Winchesters as they finished securing the animals, and Bart looked for Jim among the men. He too had pulled out the Winchester and was standing now with it butt-down, peering in the direction of the smoke smell. Bart was going to say something, but Charley Lord cut across his thoughts with a suggestion.

"Fan out; commence walkin' like the soldiers do — skirmish style."

They left the horses and moved without haste. It was getting colder by the hour, which would have helped them remain awake and alert if they hadn't just now found an even more compelling reason to be alert. If that dying fire belonged to four outlaws, what John Holbrook had said back in the yard was probably going to prove true: there was going to be trouble at the end of this trail.

It was impossible for Bart to see the most distant rider, and since there was no sound, he had to guess that the farthest man would be able to make out his nearest companion and would not get too far ahead.

Charley Lord was discernible on Bart's right, walking with his carbine slung in the bend of one arm, head up and moving. Beyond Charley it was possible to make out the next man only when starlight bounced off the barrel of his carbine.

He wondered where Jim was. He did not worry about Jim doing anything that might alert the sleeping men up ahead and southward. He had seen the young Indian in situations that had required a good head, and the boy had not once made a mistake. But a sixteen-year-old with a carbine in a situation that was probably going to be a lot worse before it got any better, was not something Bart Templeton felt comfortable about.

Finally, the scent of smoke grew stronger. It no longer came and went with the moving air, which meant the riders were on the right course. At least until they got farther along, but smoke spread widely; they could be as much as three-quarters of a mile above or below the camp.

What resolved this issue for them was the fact that this far south there was more brush and rocks than horse-feed. What feed there was grew in clumps; tufted low hummocks which put up only a few stalks per clump, and the clumps were scattered. A grazing animal would have to cover considerable ground to get enough. Bart had paused to kneel and sky-lone the onward territory. He detected movement some distance ahead but could make out nothing except that it was much too large to be a man. He arose, closed with the range-boss, and pointed without saying a word.

As they advanced, their presence was detected. The large moving creature stopped dead-still. It was one of Alex Smith's big bay horses.

The condition of the big horse would have brought tears to its owner. It was scratched and cut. It was tucked up from being unable to eat, and when it put its big head down for Bart to rub, the dark eyes were listless.

Charley glided away to warn the other men they had found one of the stolen horses, and from this point on, to move very slowly and be particularly quiet.

As Bart started past the big horse, he was

coldly angry. There was no reason under the sun to abuse an animal as that big, gentle horse had been abused.

Charley was back in place, now holding his Winchester in two hands across his body. The smoke scent was stronger. Bart flagged for Charley to bend more northward, which he did. Moments later they came upon the other big horse and two of Bart's animals. They were in no better condition than the first horse had been in. Bart's anger increased.

They walked up a gentle low incline, beyond which it was possible to see three large old shaggy trees. Cottonwoods, but they were unable to make that out until they breasted the low roll of land. Now, the smoke scent was very clear.

There were thick, tangled stands of blue thistle and ripgut grass in the shallow low place. There was also the smell of water. Bart grounded his saddlegun and sank to one knee leaning on it as he studied the grassy place. The cottonwood trees were clearly identifiable to the west, perhaps a hundred feet from the low place. Cottonwoods did not grow where there were no shallow underground supplies of abundant water. He had never seen this particular place before and did not recall now whether he had ever seen the big trees before. He was looking down into the wide, low place whose faint, cherry-glow brilliance would not have been as noticable if the night had not been as dark as it was.

They had located the source of the smoke scent. He caught Charley's attention. When they were kneeling together, Bart said, "See if you can get someone around the low place and back about where those trees are."

Charley nodded, then asked a question. "Did you make out any bedrolls?"

Bart hadn't. "I'll bet you a new hat they're down there, though. Somewhere in that tall grass and whatnot. A damned buffalo could bed down in that kind of growth and be invisible in broad daylight."

Charley slipped away, and Bart continued to kneel until his concentration was broken when a human voice made a wet sound somewhere up ahead in the tall undergrowth, coughed, and lustily expectorated.

Bart exhaled soundlessly. John Holbrook's guess had been right. Even thought the horse thieves were down in that tangle somewhere, it was not going to be a simple thing to get at them.

Charley returned, jutted his jaw in the direction of the trees, and said, "Sent one man. Your kid went with him."

When Bart looked up sharply, Charley saw the look and spread his hands. "Cuff wanted him along and he wanted to go. Don't worry, there are no slugs in his carbine, and Cuff will watch out for him. Now then, how do we get down in there and catch these bastards without rousing them up?"

Bart said, "Crawl. But you better bring in the men north of you so we can be together down in there — and stay together — so we don't shoot each other."

Charley scuttled away again. In his absence Bart considered the low place from the standpoint of men trying to escape from it. If they tried it, they would be on foot — if they didn't get shot trying. Men on foot in this kind of country could be walked down by mounted men with very little effort.

With one loaded Winchester and one unloaded one across where those shaggy trees were, there would be no escape in that direction, so all he had to worry about was someone escaping either southward or northward. As Charley came back with two riders, Bart had completed his plan. He told the two rangemen to crawl into the tangled undergrowth to the north. He and Charley Lord would do the same at the southward end. One of the cowboys said, "If there's a fight down in there, and those fellers over by the trees open up, a man could end up in hell a lot earlier than'd ought to."

Charley wagged his head at the cowboy. "You know who's over there, Fred. The only way Cuff will fire is if someone jumps out of that place and runs toward him."

The rider named Fred did not look entirely mollified, but when his companion brushed his arm and turned northward, Fred went with him.

Charley leaned and said, "He's a good hand, but so help me, no matter what he's told to do, he's always got to come up with a damned argument."

Bart nodded absently. He was trying to imagine where those outlaws would have bedded down in relation to the dying campfire. Ordinarily, particularly in a country with cold nights, men rolled in close to the fire. Bart thought this was where they would find the outlaws as he jerked his head for Charley to follow him, and started crawling.

They encountered mosquitos about the time they reached the first damp soil with its tangle of weeds, grass, and struggling little cottonwood shoots. Hungry mosquitos. Charley Lord cursed under his breath and finally paused long enough to turn up his collar and button it. That helped but these were very enterprising mosquitos, perhaps because they were also not particularly well fed ones. Wild game no doubt came to the sump-spring for water, but for the most part wild game was protected by fur.

Bart brushed the pests away with his hand, thrust into the tall undergrowth, felt his hands and knees turn chilly with water, and looked back. Charley was coming but more slowly. Since it was improbable that the outlaws had bedded down on wet ground, Bart guessed they would be across the low place, over where the ground sloped slightly upward, toward the trees. He set a direct course in that direction and got steadily wetter until he came out where the spring actually was.

The water smelled sour this deep into the morass, except where it came sluggishly out of the earth. There, although it looked dark, it was probably safe to drink. He encountered a variety of animal tracks and more hungry mosquitoes. When he looked back, he saw Charley yanking his hat down over his ears with one hand and holding his carbine out of the mud with the other hand.

Unexpectedly, a horse whinnied somewhere behind them to west. Bart had to drop flat in the mud. He heard nothing for a full minute, then a man seemed to rise up out of the ground about seventy-five feet from him, across the high, rank undergrowth. All he could make out of the man was his chest, shoulders, and head. He stood for a long time staring in the direction of that horse sound. When it was not repeated, the man turned to look southward and northward, then sank down out of sight.

Bart craned around. Charley was also hidden by the wild growth, on his belly in the mud. He saw Bart looking back and wagged his head in disgust.

Crossing around the sump-spring was not particularly difficult, except that Bart could not see ahead, and it was muddy traveling. When he finally felt the ground beginning to lose most of its stickiness, he raised up very cautiously until he could see through the tall weeds and grass stalks.

There were two bedrolls up ahead where the ground was high enough to be dry. He sat on his haunches like a rodent, wondering what had motivated those horse thieves to sleep down where there were hoards of mosquitoes when, if they had gone back as far as the cottonwoods, they probably would not have encountered any; certainty not as many.

He looked back. Charley was watching him. He dropped down and resumed crawling across the worst of the mud to ground that was not dry, but that was more firm than it had been behind him.

There was not a sound. He had not thought about the men waiting among the cottonwoods or the men crawling into the low place from the north. When he pushed carefully ahead, using his carbine barrel to ease aside the tangled undergrowth, a frog as large as a man's hand sprang up in alarm, bounced off Bart's chest, and went floundering in the direction of the water. He stopped and allowed a moment for his heart to resume its normal cadence.

The place where the frog had been was eaten off to within six inches of the ground. A hungry horse had probably done that, until tormenting mosquitoes drove him away.

Now, Bart could see those two bedrolls clearly. There were men in them, hats on their heads and bandanas up over the lower parts of their faces. The mosquitoes did not have much area to maneuver in. Both bedrolls had Winchesters lying atop saddleboots less than six inches distant. There were also a pair of coiled gunbelts even closer to the sleeping men, holsters up and gun butts arranged for instant gripping.

The guns worried Bart less than the other two bedrolls. He risked rocking back and sitting up on his haunches again in order to find them. He was successful. The other two horsethieves were farther up the slope, lying about a hundred feet from each other. From up there, if those two men sat up, they would be able to see everything happening down closer to the soft ground.

Bart crawled back to Charley. "Two in front of me. We can take care of them, but the other two are farther up the slope, an' we can't reach them, there is no cover for us to use crawling up there, and if we make any sound at all taking out the first two, those bastards will wake up sure as hell. They have a clear view of the whole sump area."

Charley's response was consistent with his mood. "Naturally. You sure didn't expect this to be easy; it hasn't been since we tied the horses and struck out on foot. All right. I can crawl back the way we came, sneak plumb around and get over to the cottonwoods. Cuff can slither down to the edge of the slope and wait for those outlaws down below to sit up — and blow their scalps off."

Bart did not see any alternative, but he did not like making Charley crawl back again, so he said he would go, and the rangeboss placed a muddy hand on Bart's shirtfront and shook his head. "I'll do it, only that leaves you in here to face two of them."

Bart was not very worried. "I can take care of one of them by the time the other one wakes up ... I hope I can anyway. Good luck, Charley."

The rangeboss grunted and turned back

through the mud. Bart watched him briefly before going back toward that grazed-off place where he had an unobstructed sighting of the two bedrolls. He thought it had been one of these men he had seen stand up when the horse had whinnied. That probably meant at least one of those horse thieves was a very light sleeper.

He wiped off the carbine as well as he could, looked left and right, then eased out of the dense undergrowth into the grazed-off place. He knew he should wait until Charley got to the trees, but darkness was not going to last much longer. Once there was even the faintest hint of dawn, his presence, and the presence of the two riders northward somewhere, would be detectable by the outlaws. He had no doubt that as soon as it was light enough for a man to see his hand in front of his face, the horse thieves would be up and moving.

CHAPTER 12
BAD LIGHT

He had quite a distance of grazed-off stubble to cross before he could reach the pair of sleeping men. If he decided to make a more cautious approach by going far above — or below — the grazed-off place, he might have been able to approach the bedrolls with less danger of discovery, but he might still be down on all fours crawling along when false-dawn appeared.

The hell with caution. He dried the carbine again, wiped both hands and started forward. The smoke scent was strong. It mingled with the other aroma which was peculiar to this area — stagnant water.

There was not a sound until to the north somewhere something scuttling swiftly through the undergrowth shook bushes and bent grass. Bart ground his teeth, rocked back aiming his saddlegun, waiting for the light sleeper to pop up again. He didn't and the distant sound died.

Bart's heart recovered and he started forward, crawling until he was about thirty feet from the nearest bedroll and then pausing for a close-up examination before moving soundlessly to his left in order to arrive on the left-hand side of the nearest bedroll.

The sleeping man was completely hidden except for a thatch of coarse, awry black hair. Bart put down his Winchester, drew his side-arm, studied what little of the outlaw's head he could see in order to determine which way the man was facing, and lifted the covering blanket and canvas with his left hand. Quickly, he brought the gunbarrel down hard with his right hand and saw the outlaw's body abruptly stiffen like a coiled spring, then go slack.

Bart leaned over, got the man's weapons, put them behind him and started around in the direction of the second man. He was hoping the second soundless attack would go off as well as the first one had.

It didn't.

Up the slope where the most distant outlaws were sleeping, a nightbird squawked — perhaps because it had detected stealthily crawling men heading toward the lip of the slope from the base of the cottonwood trees.

Bart froze, turned to stare northward, and when neither of those bedrolls up there showed any life, turned back. The man he had been stalking was awake, watching Bart with black-eyed intensity as he stealthily groped on his right for the holstered six-gun he had placed there. This one was evidently the outlaw who slept like a bird.

Bart remained on all fours but rocked back enough to raise his gunhand. He did not say a word, simply aimed at the dark man's chest and waited.

The outlaw's arm stopped moving, his dark face remained fixed in Bart's direction. Bart whispered to him. "Put your hand back — outside the bedroll."

The horse thief obeyed, continuing to stare. Only once did his gaze flicker. That was when he darted a glance at the other bedroll, which was behind Bart. If his companion over there awakened, he would shoot the stranger in the back. But the bedroll was utterly still.

Bart crawled closer — close enough to see that the man he was facing was an Indian. He whispered again. "Roll over — your back to me."

The horse thief had been awakened in such a manner that his mind was instantly clear. He did not start to obey for several seconds, then he grunted around, and Bart moved to within arms length and raised the six-gun.

The bedroll came alive as the man inside it lunged desperately upward, flinging his blankets and canvas ground cloth into the air. The man was moving frantically, trying with his right hand to grasp the saw-handled butt of his holstered Colt, with his left hand pushing hard against the ground for enough leverage to get clear.

Bart sprang, chopping downward with the gunbarrel as he moved. He did not seem to have connected, but it was impossible to be sure of that because of the wadded bedding which absorbed his blow. The gun had not been cocked and now there was no time. The Indian was hampered in his attempt to get both feet squarely set for a leap, but he had reached the gun. Bart launched himself at the man, struck him in the back knocking him forward, face first.

The Indian clutched his gun even as he instinctively flung both arms foward to break the fall which drove him into the ground. Bart clubbed at the man's gun arm, struck it hard twice before the outlaw arched his back like a bucking horse to throw Bart off.

They came around on all fours like fighting roosters, but the Indian's arm had been injured. He tried to move fast and twisted in an effort to raise the gun. The arm moved but awkwardly and slowly.

Bart lashed out with his left hand, felt the outlaw's cheekbone under his fist, and with his right hand struck violently at the rising gun. He missed the weapon but connected with wrist-bone. The gun flew out of the Indian's grip. He pulled his right arm in, cradling it to his body with his left hand as he said, "No more."

From up the slope in sooty gloom a troubled voice said, "Hey, Axel, you'n him stop that damned fighting."

Bart jutted his gun. In a whisper he said, "Tell him, 'all right.'"

The Indian obeyed, but now the second outlaw up there was awake and his temperament was different. He snarled at the man beside him. "I told you ten times they wasn't worth the powder to blow them to hell."

The first one's retort was testy. "All right. When we needed two more men, where was I supposed to find them? They don't grow on trees, dammit . . . Frank, it's time to get up anyway. Dawn's coming."

Bart and the injured Indian faced one another, silent and waiting. Bart finally jerked his head and gestured with his gun for the Indian to walk down toward the wet ground. As the Indian started to obey by arising, Bart whispered to him. "Tell them you'll go bring in the horses."

Without even a quaver in his voice the Indian obeyed, then he and Bart stood up and went threshing back down through the soggy underbrush and ripgut.

Daylight was coming, but as yet visibility was not good enough for the arguing horse thieves up the slope to be able to discern that Bart was not one of them.

They were still arguing, their voices increasingly knife-edged, when behind them atop the lip of land someone said, "Shut up!" The men in their bedrolls were stunned. Both craned to look backward and upward. Two Winchesters were pointing directly at them, but the men behind them were little more than dark humps.

Lower down someone was groaning in his soogans. Up the slope no one paid any attention to that. The outlaw with the angry disposition said, "What'n'ell do you think you're doin' up there?"

The reply he got was equally ornery: "We was waitin' for the Second Coming up here, that's what we was doing. Now then, both you gents come up out of them bedrolls like you was snakes shedding their skin, and the first man who even looks at them guns is never goin' to leave this place. Not for all Eternity. Come out — careful now."

Under the circumstances the advice had been very good, but the man with the angry disposition was more than enraged; he was desperate. As far as he knew they were a hundred miles from a settlement. Out here where the law was swift with its illegal justice, he was convinced that regardless of subsequent events he and his companions were going to be killed.

He had lost friends that way. He had come within an ace of also being killed a number of times. He did not need to have the men aiming weapons at him identify themselves. They were stockmen and they were his enemies. He began working his way up out of the bedroll as he had been ordered to do. He looked down where the Indian had gone for the horses. There was no help there. He looked to his right. Jake was doing the same, he was pushing himself up out of the bedroll like a moth coming out of its cocoon. He pushed with short strokes until his right hand was about even with the wrapped shell belt with the holster on top. He pushed a little more, glanced again at his companion, twisted harder to see up the slope. The Winchesters were still there, but it was too darkly gloomy for him to make out the men holding them, which was fine because that meant they could see him no better.

He pulled down a big breath and held it as he used his left arm to push with so the men on the land above would see that he was still coming out of the soogans, and felt swiftly and surely for the cold gun butt with his right hand. He gave one more shove with his stiff left arm, then rolled with the hammer rising under his thumb. He fired directly at the gun pointing squarely at him, and rolled frantically. His bullet struck steel and made a screaming sound as it shattered and whined away in pieces.

Beside him Jake was still climbing out, but the moment he fired, Jake dropped and rolled sideways. There was no return fire. There was now just one gunbarrel up there. As the angry man rolled, he snapped off a shot at that gun too, and knew he had missed even before the red-orange muzzleblast with its accompanying deafening sound of an explosion came and went.

He sprang up into a crouch and ran northward, weaving and ducking. Jake had his gun, too, and fired wildly as he also got to his feet and ran, but in the opposite direction, southward. Jake ran directly into someone's Winchester. The flame limned him for a second, arms upflung, head back, knees curling outward. Then the light was gone and Jake was flat down and utterly still. A man shouted. He had a powerful voice, which he'd developed over a lifetime of shouting at cattle. Charley Lord could be heard for a half mile when he shouted like that. "Got one! Cuff, you all right?"

There was no answer, but lower down the man who had been groaning had crawled out of his bedroll. In his frantic desperation he crawled over his guns before realizing what they were. He twisted for the handgun, got up holding it and went charging down across the muddy place.

The pair of Holbrook riders who had been stationed to the north of the sump-spring could skyline the crouching, fleeing man because there was finally just enough dawn-light for that. Neither one of them called for him to stop; they both fired at the same time. The stumbling man out in the swamp-like tangled undergrowth was punched so hard sideways that both his arms flew over his head before he disappeared in the undergrowth.

The angry man got clear of the low place and hesitated to look back. He had seen some-one go down out near the sump-spring, and he had seen twin flashes where the men who had shot him were crouching in the weeds. He raised his six-gun with methodical care and fired once in that direction, then ran east-ward, able to stand erect now and cover ground rapidly.

The low place became unnaturally silent. One of the two Indian horse thieves was out there lying dead in the mud, and up where the ground was harder southward, there was another dead man — Jake.

Bart shoved his captive to the ground with considerable force when the firing started, then got belly-down himself as he turned to look back. The Indian horse thief was less concerned about the shooting than he was about the man who had captured him. He thought he had a broken arm, but he still had one usable arm. He narrowed his eyes to pull in more light and looked for Bart's gunhand. It was in the grass where his captor was still leaning as he looked back.

The Indian ignored the shouting and confusion and shifted his weight to be ready to roll up to his feet the moment he snatched the gun away from his captor.

Bart was concentrating on the firing. He heard Charley Lord's shout, saw the distant flash where the angry man had fired, and with a sudden intuitive warning swung his head toward the Indian nearby, who was rising up off the ground with the aid of one arm, twisting as he came up in order to be in a position to lunge for the Colt.

Bart started to move about the same time the Indian kicked savagely and swung his thick body sideways to pin Bart's gunhand to the ground.

It was an act of pure desperation. The kind of thing a man would do who was perfectly satisfied that unless he could escape, he was going to be killed.

Bart wrenched his arm away as the horse thief came down on him. He rolled and brought up a knee. The Indian's air burst out in raw agony when the knee connected, but he still struggled. Bart punched him twice, got clear of him and got to his feet as he cocked the six-gun. They looked steadily into one another's eyes in the fishbelly cold light.

Bart let his breath out and gestured. "Stand up. Now walk, you son of a bitch."

The Indian could not straighten up. He crab-walked and that too was very painful, but he neither made a sound nor looked around at the man driving him from behind.

Charley Lord yelled again. "Bart? You all right?" He also called to the men who had been fired upon at the north end of the low place. They answered him. So did Bart. He did not take his eyes off the injured outlaw when he asked about Cuff and Jim Moore. This time when Charley answered it was with less of a roar. "The boy's all right, but Cuffs bleedin' bad. His carbine come back and hit him in the face. Bart?"

"Yeah?"

"I'll stay with him. You fellers can bring

167

the horses around here."

Bart was heading in the direction of their horses when the pair of Holbrook riders who had been fired upon by the angry man walked out of the pearling light. He turned his Indian outlaw over to them and started around the low place toward the distant cottonwood trees.

He had not gone more than ten yards when someone up ahead of the pair of Holbrook riders and the Indian fired. Bart winced at the unexpected sound and turned back. Both the Holbrook riders were firing back from the ground. But whoever had fired at them from farther out did not fire again.

When Bart reached them, the Holbrook men were on their feet but the captive Indian outlaw was not. One of the riders stepped over and nudged him with a boot toe. The Indian was dead.

Bart put up his gun and knelt. The Indian had been struck squarely in the center of the forehead.

As Bart was rising he looked ahead where visibility was increasing but was still a long way from being very good. The riders had been herding the Indian ahead of them. Whoever had been able to see them coming and had fired, had aimed at the first dark silhouette he had been able to make out.

He was still out there, somewhere. Bart told the riders to leave the Indian and go far northward, then come down in the direction of the horses. Then he changed his mind and sent one of them back toward the cottonwood trees to stay with Charley and Cuff while he and the remaining rider made the northward sashay. What worried Bart was that the escaping horse thief would continue running east. With dawn close, unless the outlaw changed course, he would eventually see the tethered horses. If he got astride, he probably would escape.

He and the rider with him trotted. They had to cover a lot of ground while the man they knew was out there only had to continue going in a straight line to find what to him would be a god-send — saddle horses without riders.

The cowboy said, "I seen him shoot up the bank. Then he ran northward. We couldn't get in a shot because he kept bobbing and changing course. He got past an' behind us, and when we shot that feller in the low place, this other feller shot at us from behind."

Bart conserved his breath by not commenting. They had covered about half the distance when the cowboy spoke again. "I'll tell you one thing for a fact; he's got no more'n two slugs left in his gun. Maybe only one."

Bart changed course slightly when he could make out the distant clump of brush where they had left the horses. He could not make out the animals until they were closer and coming down toward the buckbrush from the north.

Then he saw that the animals were standing stiffly erect and staring slightly southward, their attention being held by something they had seen.

Bart changed course again, slackened his gait a little, and led the cowboy past the buckrush, past a jumble of waist-high rocks, and turned west when he had the big thicket between himself and the horses.

His carbine was back where the fight had started and right now he wished he had it. Handguns were not exactly worthless at any considerable range, but they were a lot less accurate than a Winchester.

He halted behind the big, flourishing thicket where he and his companion could hear the horses moving uneasily on the far side. The cowboy brushed Bart's arm and jerked his head. "I'll go around from here."

Bart nodded and turned in the opposite direction. He was down where the big bush rounded a little when he thought he heard leather grate over rock.

He sank low to peer out beyond the bush.

This was an area of infrequent but abundant stands of underbrush. The man who came stealthily around from behind a smaller thicket was moving on the balls of his feet. He had no hat, his hair was awry, and he was holding a cocked six-gun out front.

The stranger eased one foot ahead and that same sound of leather rubbing stone came like a faint whisper through the utter silence and stillness of oncoming dawn.

The man was watching the saddled horses, and they were watching him. Beyond them, northward, the Holbrook rider moved past his shielding brush and was seen instantly by the man stalking the horses, who snapped off a thunderous shot that made every tethered horse sitback on his tied reins in panic.

Bart came upright very slowly, aimed and fired. The stalking man had seconds to turn a coarse, beard-stubbled face in Bart's direction, surprise etched deeply upon it, before his legs sprung and he fell.

CHAPTER 13
MEN ON HORSEBACK

Dawnlight had the texture of gray flint, and until the sun arrived the day was cold and still. Cuff's nose had been badly lacerated but it was not broken. He had several additional cuts and some purpling bruises. He looked much worse than he could have been from those facial injuries. He was in pain, his features were lop-sided with swellings, and his eyes barely showed through. What might have helped was whiskey, of which they had none. His shirt and trousers were soaked scarlet, and after the men made him as comfortable as they could over where the ground was dry on the western lip of the low place, they left Jim Moore with him, led saddle horses down into the mud, and retrieved the first dead horse thief. By the time they had them all, the sun was up. It washed away the dismalness, but when the men went after the loose horses and returned with four more than they had come down there to find, it required another hour to bring in the saddles, get them rigged out, and relash the dead outlaws across the horses' backs.

When they got strung out to start back, Bart kept Jim Moore up in front with him. Some of Cuffs blood had splattered on the youth, and he had turned his back as the dead men had been boosted up and tied into place.

He was silent for an hour. Bart did not press him. Mr. Holbrook's statement had proved true in the worst way. Even an Indian youth who had grown up in the presence of death would not have been prepared for what had happened back at the sump-spring.

Jim looked steadily ahead where the recovered horses plodded along, rested but still lethargic. Bart glanced back occasionally. Charley Lord rode on one side of Cuff, and another man rode upon the opposite side, but it did not appear to Bart Templeton that Cuff was likely to faint and fall. He looked like the wrath of God, but he sat loosely erect in his saddle, in full control.

There was a little conversation for the first couple of miles, then it dwindled as the tension faded. For a while no one seemed to think about the miracle which had brought every one of them through that vicious fight alive, and with only one injury. That would come later.

Bart, buttoned up to the gullet, tugged a

time or two at his roping gloves and watched the new day arrive a little at a time, almost grudgingly. He was tired, filthy, sore all over, and as reaction set in, he also became doggedly silent. He and Jim Moore had been a long while without rest. They were both functioning on a reserve of strength that would not last much longer.

The boy glanced at the man beside him, then turned forward again without speaking. Bart could feel the boy's distress and bewilderment. Jim did not ride back as straight-up in the saddle as he had coming down into this country, and he did not once look at the Winchester beneath his leg.

The sun was climbing, there was morning heat, and before long they would be able to see the Holbrook rooftops, before Bart said, "Bad."

Jim Moore turned to face him and nodded.

"Nothing good ever comes out of stealing — horses or anything else. They didn't help matters by making a war out of it."

Jim rode along in silence.

"Two of them were whites an' two were Indians."

Jim responded to that. "Mr. Lord told me. He told me to stay with Cuff, that way I wouldn't have to look at them."

Bart spat aside and considered the slightly

174

bobbing ears of the horse he was riding. "Cuff got pretty badly hurt."

"Yes. There was blood like someone had cut the throat of a deer. Some of it splattered on me. I've bled out animals. It never bothered me. I never saw a man bleed out before."

Bart smile. "You've had to grow up pretty fast, Jim."

The youth was watching the far flow of open country and said nothing.

Charley Lord rode up. He was smoking a brown paper cigarette which surprised Bart, who had never seen Charley use tobacco before. At the look he got, Charley removed the quirley, gazed at it, then lifted his eyes to Templeton's face. "I used these things years ago, then quit when I was sick for ten days and just never started up again until this morning." Charley smashed the cigarette atop his saddlehorn and dropped it. He grinned. "All right, I'm ready to go another five years without 'em. I guess it was being fired-up for so long back there. Sort of shreds a man's nerves."

Bart's expression had not been critical, just interested. He did not pursue the subject.

Charley had ridden up because he had been thinking about the dead men. "They most likely are worth some bounty money, Bart. They sure as hell wasn't on their first raid, judgin' from the looks and the age of them."

"You'd have to take them over to town and hunt up Deputy Morris, have him identify them, find out where they're wanted."

The rangeboss had already thought of that. "Or have whoever takes the supply wagon in tomorrow tell Morris what we got, and he can ride out."

Bart had not known the supply wagon was going to head for town tomorrow. There was no reason that he should have known. He nodded his head, "Yeah, or do something like that. But you can't have them above ground too long."

Charley nodded; he knew that. "You'd ought to be put in for at least a quarter of the bounty, Bart."

"Not me. It's bad enough having to live with a killing, justified or not. Accepting money for it would make it a lot harder to live with."

The rangeboss drifted away. Jim Moore gazed at Bart from an expressionless face and said nothing.

Alex Smith's big horses were stretching for grass-heads as they walked along. So were the other animals. The burdened horses would have, too, if they'd been able to. They were in no better condition than the loose horses.

They could see the rooftops in the distance

when Jim Moore said, "Mr. Smith isn't goin' to like the looks of his horses."

That was a statement that required no answer, but Bart wanted to keep the boy talking so he agreed. "Yep. But at least he'll get them back, an' he can take them home and spend a couple of months getting them back into shape. That part he'll be happy about."

Jim was watching the big horses plod along. "Indians use horses, they don't make pets of them."

Bart answered very dryly. He had seen how Indians used horses. "Yes, I know. But most Indians got families. Alex doesn't even have a wife, let alone kids, so those big horses are his family."

Jim seemed to have no difficulty with this. He'd once had a brindle dog. They had been inseparable right up to the day his dog stepped into someone's wolf trap and bled to death before he was found.

Charley sent a rider ahead to the yard so there would be hot water and clean cloth to bathe Cuff's face with. It was too much to hope that Dr. Mailer would be visiting from Holtville. He did visit, and quite often, but without a predictable schedule.

They would probably have to send Cuff to town tomorrow with the supply wagon. It would be a long, uncomfortable trip. Sixty miles just one way with a team and wagon took two days. And two days back. Coming back probably wouldn't be so bad; Dr. Mailer could dose Cuff with a painkiller, the way he had done last year when he had operated on John Holbrook's back to remove that little obsidian arrowpoint he had been carrying around in his vertebra for half his lifetime. Doc Mailer was very good at his trade. If anyone could patch Cuff up, he could.

Heat was coming, and there was no little wind as there usually was on this kind of a day. Bart glanced up. Another of those thin veils of filmy obscurity was stretching across the sky. The last time there had been one of those things up there it hadn't rained even though the general opinion was that those filmy overcasts meant rain was on the way. Maybe it wouldn't rain this time either, but the land certainly needed rain. It needed it every couple of weeks all summer long to keep the feed green and strong, but it never rained like that. Mostly, when it did rain, there might be deluge overnight and not another drop for two months.

Jim Moore spoke. "After your wife and the others come home are you going back to the big mesa?"

Bart thought over his reply. "I suppose so, but maybe not for a while. We just went up there to see if the bands were still there. We didn't figure to trap any. Not for maybe another few weeks."

"Does your wife help you trap wild horses?"

This required more pondering. "She never has, but then we've only been married about a year. I expect she will when we go up there again in a few weeks."

"Is your wife Indian?"

Bart turned his head slowly. By nature Indians were direct, not given to subtlety. "Part," he replied. "Her mother was Indian."

Jim inclined his head as though Bart's answer had confirmed something for him. "What kind of Indian?"

"Tell you what, Jim, when we get this mess all settled, why don't you sit down with her and talk. She'd like that. She likes you."

"Did she tell you that?"

"Yes."

"I like her. I think she's the best-lookin' woman I ever saw."

Bart's eyes crinkled. He said, "Jim, did you know that you and I are a lot alike?"

"No," Jim said, puzzled before he got Bart's meaning. Then he smiled.

Charley Lord loped past in the direction of the yard. It was possible finally to see activity up there. The rider he had sent ahead had undoubtedly told his tale. Bart watched the rangeboss and when they were a little closer he and Jim Moore began easing up alongside the loose horses so they could be herded into one of the big pole corrals up ahead. Behind them the rangemen still plodded along, slack shanks from their saddlehorns to the bits of the led-animals with their unfeeling, swaying cargo.

Bart and the others were silent, peering ahead to see what was happening in the yard. Clearly, there was a bustle of activity. Apparently John Holbrook, in the absence of his rangeboss and riding crew, had gotten the wood makers down off Wild Horse Mesa by himself, because Bart saw the old running gear of Abel Morrison's wagon with its load of dry logs in the middle of the yard.

Jim jutted his chin in the direction of the wagon. "How did they get down without the big horses?"

"Mr. Holbrook's got big harness horses, too."

"Mr. Holbrook is your wife's father?"

"Yes."

"Do you like him?"

"Yes, indeed. You will, too, when you get to know him."

"I won't get to know him unless he comes up where my camp is, and I don't think he would do that."

Bart glanced at the boy's profile and said nothing. Eventually he waved Jim farther to their right so he could turn the loose horses in the direction of the wide-open gate of the big gathering corral. Jim reined clear, then came in from the drag. It was simply a matter of showing the horses where they were supposed to go. They were too worn down to do anything other than obey.

As the animals scuffed dust passing through the gate Alex Smith appeared, accompanied by Abel Morrison and Foster Bullard. Alex got his first good look at his big horses as they listlessly plodded past. He let out a groan that could be heard by the riders entering the yard from a different direction with the led-horses. Then he ran through the dust and ducked inside the corral as Bart swung off to close the gate. He went from one horse to the other passing his hands over their injuries. He did not make another sound until he had thoroughly examined both horses, then he turned toward Bart and walked forward as he said, "Where are they? Where are the sons of bitches that treated my horses like that?" He pushed the gate open, walked through, and left it to Bart to close the gate, pushing back his old coat to expose the holstered Colt, his eye searching among the dismounted men for strangers.

Jim Moore ran after him, caught his sleeve and tugged. "They're dead," he said. "That's them bein' led toward the barn."

Alex turned and looked fiercely at the youth. "How many was there?"

"Four. Two Indians an' two white men."

"They're all dead, Jim?"

"Yes. They was all killed down where we caught up with them."

Alex stood a moment gazing at the youth, then faced in the direction the burdened horses were being led. John Holbrook was walking with them. His riders were bringing up the rear, leading their tired horses. Alex very slowly yanked his coat free and let it drop back to cover the holstered Colt.

Bart led his horse and Jim's animal toward the rear entrance of the barn to be off-saddled and put into stalls until their sweaty backs were dry, because although that filmy overcast prevented the sun's full rays from reaching the earth, there was still more than enough sunlight to scald the backs of horses which were dark with salt-sweat.

There was only a little conversation while the riders cared for their animals, but when the paunchy *cocinero* appeared in the doorless front barn opening to announce that he'd had stew simmering in thick gravy all

182

morning, and six crab apple pies he had baked yesterday waiting for anyone who was hungry, the talk became more lively. There was even some relieved laughter as the men finished their chores and went straggling across the yard, carrying the Indian youth with them.

That left Bart Templeton and John Holbrook to unload the dead men, lay them out side by side in a cool, dark place, and cover them with wagon canvas.

CHAPTER 14
A DISCOVERY

When Bart entered the main house behind his father-in-law, the aroma of cooking almost overwhelmed him, and when his wife appeared in the kitchen doorway, he felt his weariness diminish, along with the strong sensation of hunger.

She went into his arms. He held her very close. Her father turned his back on them in embarrassment, marched to the sideboard to pour whiskey into a pair of glasses, and turned back when Nan herded them both into the kitchen to listen to what her husband had to say while she simultaneously kept an eye on the stove.

He told them everything in detail. During pauses he sipped whiskey with predictable results, since he had not eaten in a long time. His wife noticed the signs. She immediately filled two plates with food and placed them in front of her husband and her father. While they were eating, she discreetly removed the whiskey glasses.

After supper Bart took a towel and some brown soap out to the bathhouse, soaked and scrubbed until drowsiness arrived, then dried off and, after dressing, returned to the house. His father-in-law was alone in the parlor. Nan had gone down to the bunkhouse to do what she could for Cuff. Holbrook got two more glasses of whiskey, but this time there was something down below to absorb it. Bart and his father-in-law talked for a while; then when Bart could not keep his eyes open any longer, John Holbrook accompanied him to a bedroom door and left him. When Nan returned a half hour later, her father jerked his head. "Dead to the world in your old bedroom."

Bart was not the only one who slept like a log. Down at the bunkhouse only Alex Smith remained awake, his good eye fixed on the ceiling in darkness, his heart still full of fury, but everyone else down there slept like the dead. It had been a long and arduous day for the rangemen. It had not been much easier on Foster, Alex, and Abel.

Before daylight the rangemen stirred. Across the yard the yellow glow of lamplight shone from the cook house. Charley and another rangeman went down to the barn to pitch feed and were surprised to find that someone had gotten down there before them.

It was Jim Moore. He was standing in the

poor light at the foot of the row of dead out-laws. He had pulled back the canvas a couple of feet and was standing completely still. He did not seem to hear the riders walk in.

Charley looked long at the youth, then jerked his head for the cowboy to start feeding the stock. After the rider disappeared out back with a huge flake of hay balanced over his shoulder on a three-tined fork, Charley approached the Indian boy. Jim did not move. He was staring at the dead men from a rigidly expressionless face. Charley leaned to look at him closer in the poor light. "Jim? You all right?"

He got no answer. He too looked at the dead men. They were not something even a man as seasoned and hardened as Lord was would want to gaze at very long. Yesterday, down near the battleground, he had thought of the lad when they had brought the corpses in. He had told Jim to stay with Cuff, which he did. Charley's reason was because the dead men were filthy, ragged, with dead eyes show-ing dull behind the half droop of lids. It was nothing a youngster should have to see.

By the weak light of early dawn, some of the details of violent death were mitigated but there was still blood, dried black now and caked, as was the mud. Charley shifted his weight, stood hip-shot with both thumbs hooked into his belt looking from the youth to the corpses. He sighed finally, brushed Jim's shoulder lightly, and said, "This isn't any good, son. Come along, we'll go out front and breathe fresh air."

Jim turned slowly, looking up, black eyes pain-deadened. "That one on the left, that's Axel. The one next to him. That's Johnex."

Charley nodded. He had heard the thicker of the two dead man called Axel. He stopped nodding and looked steadily at the boy. There had been no mention of the other one's name. "Jim? You knew them?"

"Yes . . . They were my brothers."

Charley raised his head, listening to the man out back pitching feed, then lowered it. "Are you plumb sure?"

"Yes."

Charley shifted stance again. "I don't recollect hearing that you had any kin. Someone said you were an orphan."

"I am. Before my mother and father died Alex and Johnex left the reservation. Maybe four years ago." Jim looked at the dead Indians again before adding, "They ain't changed. They look the same as when I last saw them."

Charley stepped ahead, leaned, and slowly drew the old wagon canvas back over the heads of the dead outlaws, and as he straightened back the chore-hand came over to them.

He had finished feeding. His gaze crossed with Charley Lord's gaze. He could feel the odd mood of the rangeboss and lifted his hat, scratched vigorously, then without a word walked out of the barn on his way to the wash rack out behind the bunkhouse.

Charley stood in thought for a while, then turned and walked out into the yard on his way over to the main house. John Holbrook admitted him with a quizzical look, Charley could see Nan and her husband in the lighted kitchen. He considered his employer from an advantage of several inches, then jerked his head and stepped away from the door. Holbrook followed, closed the door, and faintly frowned.

"Fred and I went down to feed. The In'ian boy was standing there like a statue. He'd pulled the canvas off them outlaws," stated the rangeboss.

"What the hell did he do that — ?"

"Wait, John. Let me finish. Those two horse stealing In'ians that got killed yesterday was his brothers."

Holbrook looked blank. "Brothers? He's an orphan. Nan told me that."

"Yeah. His folks are dead but his two older brothers left the reservation before they died and until this mornin' he hadn't seen them. One was called Axel. I heard someone usin' that name in the dark down where the fight started. The boy said the other one's name was Johnex."

John Holbrook looked over his shoulder in the direction of the barn. As he was turning back, the *cocinero* rang his triangle, sending bell sounds in all directions for a considerable distance. The men emerged from the bunkhouse on their way to have breakfast.

He faced his foreman as his daughter opened the door looking around for him. She smiled. "Good morning, Charley."

Charley brushed his hat brim. " 'Morning."

She turned the smile to her father. "Breakfast is ready."

Holbrook nodded. After his daughter had closed the door, he said, "Is he takin' it hard?"

Charley thought about his reply before offering it. "I'd say he is. But with them you just can't ever be dead certain. He wasn't cryin'. He was just standin' there. He didn't even hear us comin' into the barn, I don't think. Just standin' there. I'd say he's takin' it hard."

Holbrook nodded, moved toward the door, and turned to say, "Charley, take him over to breakfast. I'll tell Nan and Bart. They want to keep him."

The rangeboss nodded and started down

the steps on his way to the barn to find Jim and walk him over to the cook shack for breakfast. John Holbrook closed the main house door after himself, and for a motionless moment watched his daughter and her husband. She was at the stove; he was at the table. They had been laughing.

Holbrook went toward the lighted kitchen, avoided the quick, warm glances he got, pulled out a chair, sat down, and said, "Those dead In'ians you brought back — they are the brothers of that boy you want to take home with you."

The only sound for some seconds was the crackling of frying meat. Bart leaned with both hands clenched atop the table. "Who told you that?"

His father-in-law gave them a verbatim account of what Charley had just told him out on the veranda. Finally, he looked at his daughter. She turned slowly, like a dream-walker, turned the frying meat, stirred more pepper into the golden brown frying potatoes, and said nothing.

Bart looked up once at his wife, then back to her father again. There was no need to ask questions. He arose, dragged his hat off the rack on the back of the door, and put it on as he went through the parlor on his way outside.

Ordinarily there was not as much noise coming from the cook shack during breakfast in the morning as there was during supper-time in the evening, but usually there was some rowdiness. Not this morning; the cook shack was as quiet as a tomb.

Bart went to the barn, but there was no one there. There was only the sound of horses eating dry feed. He paused, looking left and right. There was no one in sight, so he went back to the bunkhouse, where Jim had slept last night.

He was not there; the building was empty.

He was on his away toward the cook-house when he thought he very distantly heard a moving horse. But he did not stop for that. He stopped because Charley Lord had emerged from the shoeing shed. He walked over to Bart wagging his head. "I've looked every-where."

Bart's heart sank. "For Jim?"

"Yeah. John wanted me to take him with me to the cook shack and to kind of keep an eye on him."

Bart was briefly silent, straining to pick up that moving horse sound again. He heard nothing. Charley said, "I can see now I never should have left him down at the barn. Four dead men — horse thieves or not — that's a hell of a load for even a grown man to carry, let alone a skinny orphan kid."

They parted, Charley to eat breakfast with the riders, Bart to return to the house where his father-in-law had eaten, but his wife had not, even though she was sitting at the table and had placed two laden dishes at the vacant places, one for her, one for her husband.

When Bart walked in, both Holbrooks raised searching eyes. He sat down and picked up a coffee cup as he said, "Gone, I guess. Charley's been lookin' for him and can't find him."

There was a sturdy knock on the front door. Abel Morrison was standing out there when John Holbrook opened the panel. Abel smiled feebly. "It's about the lad," he said. "Alex and I was out back putting bacon grease on his bay horses. We saw the lad lead a horse out of the barn with just a bridle on him. We didn't think much about it, but when he stepped up onto the corral stringers and vaulted over onto the horse's back I called to him. Asked where he was goin' before he'd even eaten. Didn't say a word, Mr. Holbrook. Didn't even look around to see where we was or who had called to him. Just aimed the horse north along the back of the barn and rode away."

Holbrook turned. "Bart, he's gone north on horseback."

Both the Templetons came to the door. Abel nodded solemnly at them. Then he added something else. "We didn't know about those dead In'ians bein' related to him until Charley came in a while back and told us. The riders knew, but we didn't get over there to eat until they was about finished."

Bart said, "Thanks, Abel," and moved past on his way to the corrals. Nan followed him. Her father and Abel watched them until they were lost to sight in the barn, then he faced Holbrook again and shrugged. "They'll fetch him back. Mr. Holbrook — Foster, Alex, and me is obliged for your hospitality, and for your help in gettin' us down here with the wagon. We're going to hitch up now and head for Holtville. Thanks again."

John Holbrook nodded absently, eyes fixed on the corrals out behind the barn where Bart and Nan were opening a gate to snake out a pair of saddle animals. "Glad to help, Abel. Any time."

As Abel was leaving the porch, John Holbrook leaned in the doorway. Holbrook would have liked to have gone after the lad with Bart and his daughter, but according to Doc Mailer, he was not to mount even a gentle horse for another six or eight months. Anyway, he told him as he returned to the kitchen to finish his coffee, they would not need him.

Bart and Nan would overtake the boy.

Daylight was slow arriving and that misty overcast was still up there. Now too, there was the scent of moisture in the air even though the accumulation of soiled white clouds visible to the northeast did not appear to be moving very fast, if at all.

Nan rode the flashy chestnut with the flaxen mane and tail Bart had given her before their marriage. In fact, it had been her acceptance of the horse that clinched things. She had told him her mother had once said very seriously that to accept a horse from a man was a betrothal agreement between them. Her mother had been dead many years and her father had made a kind of solemn joke out of that the horse story, but when Bart offered her the horse she accepted it and they had been married.

Her husband rode his own horse, a gelding of about sixteen hands who had once ruled a band of mares on Wild Horse Mesa. Bart had nearly been killed on that horse one time, but they worked perfectly together now, and there was no horse on either of the ranches who possessed his 'bottom,' his stamina and toughness.

They rode for a while watching fresh shod-horse marks on the ground, but after an hour they rode with their heads up. Jim was not in sight, which was odd because he had not had that big a head start, and for the most part the land ahead was open, not flat, with few trees and even less underbrush until a rider got much closer to the awesome barranca that formed the south cliff-face of the distant plateau.

Nan thought he might have seen them coming and had hidden. Bart had a different idea. "I doubt that he even thought of pursuit. I think I know him fairly well. And I've known other In'ians. He is just riding. Looking straight ahead with his mind dead-still."

"Then where is he?"

Bart swung an upraised arm. "Northeast."

Nan leaned to study the ground. "The tracks are still heading north," she said.

"Yeah, I know, but it's thirty miles to the mesa and the best way to get up atop it is that old military road Alex and his friends used. And that is northeast."

He was right. At least another few miles onward the shod-horse sign did begin to angle off toward the northeast.

Nan looked at her husband. "What can we tell him?"

He faced her thoughtfully. "We? I think it'll be you. He told me he thought you were the best-lookin' woman he had ever seen."

She stood in her stirrups to see ahead better.

"He also is interested in whether you're part Indian or not. I think you're the one he'll listen to. If he listens at all."

She settled down in the saddle. "But — I don't know what to say. I don't even know if there is anything to say. The shock must have been terrible."

Bart remained silent. They had brought nothing in their haste to leave the yard. Not even his hat, not even anything to eat. Not even a canteen.

But the Wilton's camp was close to the rough country eastward. He and Nan could perhaps get a bundle of food over there before heading up toward the old military road.

If they had to ride that far.

CHAPTER 15
"NO!"

They were following the tracks because, while they seemed to be heading in the direction of the military road, in this open country they should have had a sighting by now. Jim hadn't had more than perhaps a half hour's head start, at the very most an hour. Until they got closer to the barranca where there was scattered timber, even unmoving objects should be visible and moving ones even more so.

Bart examined the onward flow of land. There were swales, grassed-over shallow little erosion gullies, a few stands of tall, wiry brush. But he still did not believe Jim was up ahead somewhere watching them from hiding.

There was a meandering creek that came off the mesa on the east side and cut its way through stirrup-high grass. The tracks led to that place, to an opening in the screen of creek willows that lined the watercourse. They paused to let the horses drink, then plowed ahead through water above the fetlocks of their animals and to the far side where the tracks made a ninety degree turn northward.

Nan rode away from the creek a short distant and halted. She called to her husband and pointed. Jim had made good time. He was northward staying close to the willows, perhaps for shade, but just as likely to be hidden. One thing seemed sure; he was indeed heading for the big plateau where he'd had a hidden camp before the wood makers had arrived up there to tempt him with Alex's big horses.

Nan said, "The only place he has," and watched the distant rider until her husband jerked his head. "Back to the opposite side. He'll see us over here."

They recrossed the creek, turned northward, and lifted the horses into a collected lope. It was cooler beside the little waterway than it had been away from it. The only distractions were nesting blackbirds among the willows. They flew up in frantic agitation. Every few yards there were more of them. The bold ones dived at the riders, and all of them screeched at the top of their voices. Their horses were neither amused nor indifferent. Nesting blackbirds would come down fast, stab a horse in the rump with their beaks, and escape easily.

Bart ignored them while trying to estimate how much more time would elapse before

they overtook the Indian boy. He was unde-
cided in his mind whether Jim would make a
horse-race out of it when he eventually knew
they were behind him.

Nan said, "It's so sad."

Bart nodded.

"Not just this, but all the rest he's had to
live through. Bart, will we ever be able to rec-
oncile him?"

He did not know. "The best we can do is
try. I don't know anything about children,
even half-grown ones."

She eased away through the willows and
emerged on the far side where she sat stone-
still searching the shimmery distance for signs
of the rider she had seen earlier.

She saw nothing. Up where Jim should
have been there were only meandering stands
of creek willows on both sides of the creek.
She was about to return to her husband in
alarm when a horse ambled out of the willows
about a mile ahead, distinctly visible because
it was moving. But there was no one on its
back.

She returned to the west side of the creek,
her face flushed, her upper lip damp. "The
horse is grazing. There's no sign of Jim."

Bart nodded. "Resting in the shade of the
willows. Maybe he's got something to eat. It's
goin' to be a blow to his pride to have us come

up on him. Whites aren't supposed to be able to track Indians, it's supposed to be the other way around."

From this point on they walked the horses. Bart worried that if the grazing horse up yonder didn't catch the sight or smell of their horses and nicker, Jim might catch a glimpse of them moving along the west side of the creek, or he might hear them coming, although by that time, they would be very close. The ground they were riding over was slightly spongy with grass as thick as the hair on a dog's back. A herd of cattle could have trailed up the way the Templetons were doing without making a sound.

When they thought they had gone as far as they ought to on horseback, they left the animals tied and went forward on foot. Now, it was less likely that they would be seen or heard.

Bart stopped twice. Once when a dozen furious blackbirds rose into the air up ahead a fair distance, and alternately dived and screeched. He winked at Nan and covered another dozen yards, then halted again. He whispered to his wife that they had to be close, and gestured toward the angry blackbirds. She said, "I'll cross the creek. Maybe I can get close enough to catch the horse."

He did not believe her idea would work.

Even if the horse didn't see her, Jim probably would. But Bart said nothing. He just waited until she was on the far side of the watercourse, then increased his own haste in getting up where the irate birds were still diving at something on the ground among the willows he could not see, but felt certain it would be Jim.

A wood-duck made an awful squawk and sprang into the air to Bart's right where she had been sitting on eggs, already prepared to panic because she knew there was another two-legged earthbound creature no more than two or three hundred feet northward. Her courage had been dissolving ever since the first two-legged creature had arrived that close. The only thing that had kept her on the nest this long was a powerful urge to protect six fertile eggs.

Bart ignored the duck as she did not clear the top of his head by more than two feet in her clumsy, noisy fright. Jim would know something had frightened her. He widened his stride, thought he had caught a glimpse of a worn and ragged woollen sweater, and abandoned caution in favor of haste.

He came to a narrow opening among the willows, probably made by large animals coming to drink, looked across it and saw the Indian boy sitting with his head slightly cocked, listening. He saw Bart about the same time Bart saw him.

Jim sprang to his feet and spun away in the direction of the sunshine and grass where his horse had been eating. Bart plunged across the creek in pursuit. When he pushed aside the last willow on the far side, he stopped still.

Jim was standing the same way about seventy-five feet ahead. He was staring at his horse. Nan was astride it, one hand stroking the animal's neck, the other hand holding a leather belt she had fashioned into a war bridle.

She smiled as she said, "Jim, you didn't have to run away."

The boy said nothing. He did not even look around when Bart came up behind him.

Nan continued to stroke the horse when she spoke again. "Nothing will change what happened. Running to the mountains won't help. You can't run from grief any more than you can run from guilt. It runs right alongside you." She slid off the horse and walked toward the boy leaving the horse to crop grass around the part of her britches-belt that went across its lower jaw on the inside. Her eyes moved to Bart then back to Jim. She stopped fifty feet away. "Jim, you can handle grief a lot easier with people who are fond of you then you can by yourself."

Bart loosened. He had thought for a while it was going to turn into a foot race. He had not been positive he would win that kind of a match. He had seen how long and far and hard Jim Moore could run.

Bart felt rather than saw the tightness begin to leave the boy. He had been poised to run. But he still said nothing, not even when Nan walked much closer and smiled with her liquid black eyes, the same color eyes that the boy had. "Did Alex say anything to you?"

The boy's gaze wavered. "About what?"

"About us wanting you to come live with us."

Jim said, "Why?" with the kind of abrupt directness that would have made Bart stammer. Nan answered easily. "Because we need you and I think you need us. We want you, Jim. Later, if you want to, you can leave. We won't stop you."

The boy twisted from the waist to look steadily at Bart for a long time. Bart did not smile, did not even speak, but he gravely nodded his head.

Jim faced Nan again. "Did you know they killed my brothers?"

Bart finally spoke. "Jim, the man who killed one of your brothers was one of the other horse thieves. Your brother was walking in front of two of Mr. Holbrook's men.

That dead man back in the barn with the ginger whiskers, he . . . you remember how dark it was . . . he must have thought the man walking ahead was one of us. He shot your brother."

"How do you know that's how it happened?"

"Because I was there. I saw it, and later when I came around that bush where we'd left the horses, there he was with a cocked gun in his hand, about to get one of the horses. He made a wild shot and I didn't."

Jim raised a hand to brush at a flying insect. He looked out at the grazing horse, then he looked northward in the direction of the distant barranca. "That was Axel," he said, "Johnex got killed too."

Bart knew he had been killed, but he had not seen the killing. "Jim, remember when we rode out of Mr. Holbrook's yard? You had a carbine and a good horse. You were riding with the rest of us, and you looked proud about that. Well, I didn't want a fight down there any more than anyone else did. We wanted the horses back, and to catch the horse thieves if we could. That's what we talked about. You were there atop the lip when one of them shot uphill and hit Cuff's gun. They made it into a fight, we didn't."

Jim turned slowly toward Bart, dark eyes

steady. "I wasn't runnin' away."

Bart made a rueful little grin. "You sure fooled me, partner."

"I wanted to go up to the mesa to my old camp for a few days."

Nan came around to them from the rear. "You can go. But I think it would be easier for you to be with others right now. For a while anyway. Then you could go back up there if you wanted to."

Jim looked at the ground and shook his head. "Alone. My father said men take their grief to the lonely places."

Nan considered the slouch and the lowered head. "Do you know why? Because not only your father but many other men think it is a weakness for men to cry. Do you think that way?"

He did not raise his head when he replied. "He said to be alone so a man can talk to spirits, his forefathers, and even to the stars because among them all up there, one star belongs to you; it is yours to look at and talk to, and if it is the right star, it will help you in everything you do."

"And to cry, Jim. To beat the ground, to let the grief come out without anyone watching."

He brought his head up, finally, and studied Nan's face for a long while before speaking again. "Is that what your mother told you?

Nan answered quietly. "She told me many things, but she died before she could tell me everything else. . . . Jim?"

"Yes."

"Won't you please come back with us?"

"No."

"All right. We know what you have to do because you just told us, but Jim — when the mourning time is over, then what?"

"Then I will bring back the horse," he said. "I didn't steal it. I just borrowed. I'll bring it back."

Bart flicked a look at his wife. They had not won. Possibly they were not supposed to win. At least the boy would come back to return the horse.

Nan started past the youth to join her husband in returning to the west side of the creek. As she passed Jim Moore she paused, kissed his cheek lightly, and smiled into his wide-open eyes, then walked down through the willows with Bart.

They were walking through willow-shadows when he said, "You left your belt back there. Your britches will fall down."

She laughed at him. "No, they won't and I didn't forget the belt. He will return it."

"You're plumb sure of that?"

"Yes. He'll return my father's horse and then he will come over to our place and give me back my belt."

"Nan, if you're wrong?"

Her dark eyes shone upon him. "I have another belt. Do you want to bet me a horse that he won't bring back the belt?"

Bart did not believe it would be returned, but that kind of a bet did not appeal to him. "No m'am I raise and break horses to sell, not to gamble with."

When they were astride, riding back the way they had come, Bart turned in the saddle, braced himself with one hand atop the cantle, and looked for a distant rider. He saw him, loping slowly northward.

CHAPTER 16
SOMETHING DIFFERENT

John Holbrook had disagreed with the notion of having the Holtville deputy ride to the ranch to look at the dead horse thieves, so they had been loaded into the supply wagon, covered, and sent to town with the cowboy named Fred, who drove, and the cowboy named Cuff whose face looked terribly lop-sided, purplish and scabbed over. Actually, Cuff felt better on the second day than he had felt on the first day. He was unhappy because he could not chew, but John Holbrook had stowed a bottle of rye whiskey in the jockey-box to tide him over — if he needed tiding over.

When Nan's father had listened to his daughter's explanation about the Indian boy, he had neither smiled nor said much, only that he would be glad to get the horse back, although if it was not returned he would not suffer much, nor would it be the first horse he had lost to Indians. His last remark to the

Templetons down by the barn as they were ready to leave was: "If he returns, it'll surprise me. Not just because he probably associates us with the death of his brothers, but because Indians don't feel required to stay in one place; they roam. That's their nature. I've been around them all my life. They're free spirits. I suppose for ten thousand years they've been wondering what's beyond the next hill. That's why the reservation system doesn't work and why it's so distasteful to them. Well, you two go on home." He looked at his daughter longest. "But don't forget I live over here."

On the ride west to Bart's horse ranch, Nan had trouble with a mild feeling of guilt. When Bart broke across her thoughts, it was as though he had read her mind. He said, "It's going to take time for him to readjust to being able to do his own bossing. He couldn't ride for so many years, once he got to depending on you, and Charley, and even me to some extent."

She quietly said, "He is not a young man."

Bart scowled at her. "Your pa?" He snorted. "John Holbrook's tougher an' younger in heart and spirit than anyone I ever knew who was half his age." The scowl smoothed. "We'll ride over."

Her mood lightened as they crossed the

unmarked boundary between her father's land and Bart's. The terrain was pretty much the same. The Templeton place was a little rougher, the buildings and yard had less shade from planted trees, the westerly flow of Templeton land was deep-soiled so grass grew well when it rained and did not freeze every night, but it did not have the same expression most Holbrook land had. John Holbrook had been on his land for a great number of years. Bart hadn't.

They were off-saddling in front of the log barn when Nan looked northward where a distant barranca appeared to rise straight up for a considerable distance before it flattened on top. "How long?" she said.

Bart shot her a look then resumed his work with the horses. "Want a guess? Ten days maybe."

She led her stripped chestnut gelding out back to the corrals. As her husband held the gate for her, she smiled at him, walked past, freed the horse and turned back to say, "If it is ten days, you'll have time to really think about it, won't you?"

They started for the house when a banner of rising dust caught Bart's eye. He stopped and turned. It was Big Ben, his remount stallion, bringing in his flock, which consisted mostly of mares, but there was also a strong percentage of colts, large and small ones.

They returned to the area of the corrals to watch Ben, with his scarred forehead and thick, arched neck stop out a ways, pass back and forth in front of the mares to impress upon them that they should not come any closer, then he whirled and trotted stiffly, head up, tail out, to the west side of the corral to make challenging sweeps for the benefit of Nan's handsome chestnut and Bart's big, somewhat rawboned, muscled up bay, both of whom were eating timothy hay off the ground and did little more than lift their eyes to watch Big Ben. Geldings were not battlers any more than they were breeders; when they did fight, it was never with the wholehearted and single-minded ferocity of stallions.

Bart laughed at Ben's antics and called to him. "You big clown — they're hungry. They don't want to steal your mares."

Ben paid no attention. He continued making passes, bolder ones as the corralled horses turned their backs on him, until the bored mares began scattering, taking their colts in different directions in search of feed.

Ben had to break it off. He could not permit his mares to separate. As he loped back to nip rumps and flash teeth with both ears pinned back and eyes flashing, the scattering animals got hurriedly back into a loose band again. Ben remained behind, nipping, until he had them heading north in a run.

Nan went out back to the wash house while Bart lighted kindling in the cook stove. Even though it was warm out, sultry warm in fact, inside the house it was chilly.

He had three colts started, a *grulla* and two bays. After they had eaten, Nan went down to the breaking corral with him. She did not make suggestions although there had been times over the last year when she'd had to bite her tongue to keep from it. As her father had warned her, most men but especially horse-breakers did not take it kindly when spectators gave advice. Especially female spectators.

Just once she had volunteered to come inside the round corral to help. His response had precluded the possibility of her ever making that offer again. It was based on something she did not completely understand, although since childhood she had never seen two men in a corral breaking the same horse.

He had not spoken condescendingly; rather he had been smiling when he said, "Sweetheart, a green horse can move almighty fast. If I'm close and got to move quick, I don't want to have to climb over you to get clear." That was the easy part to explain. The part that would have been harder to explain was that when a two hundred pound man was concentrating entirely on a wild-eyed thousand pound horse neither he nor the horse needed distraction, and it did not take much. Sometimes just a bird flying past would cause a horse to erupt into a fighting, striking, lunging half ton of deadly danger.

She had been to the corral with him many times over the past year and while she still worried — not as much as she had worried before they were married and she had lived several miles away — she had learned one thing well. Her husband did not take chances. He was never careless. However, as her father had once sagely observed, and she had heard old riders say the same thing, anyone who was around horses long enough was going to get hurt by them.

She returned to the house to start supper when he had worked both the bays, had choused them into a square corral leaving the *grulla* alone in the round corral.

He called after her that he would not be long. She threw a little wave and reached the green-wood veranda before pausing up there to turn slowly, considering the seemingly endless miles of undisturbed range country. It was late springtime, early summer. Beauty lay in every direction but the approach of dusk appeared to be hurried on this day. She looked higher. Those immense galleons of white which had been floating with incredible slowness from the northwest were beginning to merge with other fleets of immensely thick high white clouds arriving from the southwest. That filmy overcast which had been in place for several days now, was yielding to them, but she hardly noticed because daylight was fading.

Inside, with a lamp glowing in the kitchen and a fire on the hearth of the parlor, she forgot everything but the meal she was beginning to prepare. Only once did she pause, and then only briefly because she had been listening to thunder all of her life. It was usually accompanied by lightning. Not this time. The rumble seemed to roll directly overhead and die southward.

When she stepped to the veranda to look for her husband, a blinding slash of white lightning that tore apart the dusk from high above all the way down to the earth, momentarily outlined the distant barranca at the top of Wild Horse Mesa.

She saw Bart turn in front of the barn and look, then he started for the house as the first rowel-sized raindrops struck. When he reached her side, he removed his hat to consider the big drops and laughed. "Gully washer sure as hell. . . . What are you looking at?"

"Did you see that lightning strike?"

"Couldn't help but see it. I'd guess everyone for a hundred miles saw it."

She jutted her chin. "It struck on the mesa."

He dropped the hat back on, looked out there where it was no longer possible to see something thirty miles distant, and knew exactly what she had meant.

He turned her toward him by both arms. "He'll be all right. They've been through things like this for a million years. They know how to look out for themselves."

"At sixteen?"

He dropped his hands from her arms but continued to gaze at her. Ever since the idea had surfaced that they would take Jim Moore in, she had been acting like a genuine mother. He did not know much about women, but he'd spent his life around mares and cows. She wouldn't have liked the comparison, but it seemed the most natural thing in the world to him.

Mares and cows acted like this at the first hint of danger to their young. They would herd them into a sheltering bosque of timber, or down in a protected arroyo, and they would stand guard as long as the danger existed.

"Well," he said lamely, "there's plenty of timber up there, plenty of places to get shelter."

"Bart, that lightning struck up there."

The rain was coming down so hard now they had to raise their voices to each other. Some of it came on an angle to reach them beneath the veranda's overhang. He did not mind getting wet, but only if he had to. He opened the door and held it until she entered, then he closed it, and closing the door he also closed out most of the drumroll of rain.

In the kitchen she worked with her back to him. Even when she put their plates on the table, she avoided his glance. He draped his hat from the peg on the back of the door, sat down, and reached for the cup of hot black coffee.

The storm seemed to be directly above them, and the sounds he had mitigated by closing the front door came through the roof. He waited until she was seated then said, "It's been building up for days. I'd guess we're in for a real gully-washer."

She smiled a little and nodded.

They ate mostly in silence, not entirely because they would have had to almost yell to be heard, but also because she had transmitted her troubled mood, her motherly fear, to him.

After supper he stoked up the fire, took a glass of two-thirds water and one-third whiskey with him to the hearth where he stood with his back to the blaze, listening to the storm, gauging its intensity, and waiting for signs that it was moving.

But those clouds had been almost a week arriving, so there was no reason to expect them to move away any faster, especially since no wind had come with the downpour.

Nan joined him in front of the fire. The house was snug and warm, but it was human nature, perhaps something residual from prehistoric times, to back up to a hearth fire when a storm was abroad.

He offered her his whiskey glass. She declined. He sighed to himself. He did not doubt at all that the Indian boy had found a safe place from the storm's fury. At sixteen he would have. At sixteen she probably would have, too. But her solemn face and inner fear was something he felt a little of. Nor could he say anything to allay it.

He sipped, remembered how she had opened her heart to the boy, and nodded to himself about his own feelings, different from hers, but in emotion, not in substance. Jim was terribly hurt right now. A man needed to be alone. Healing took time. Maybe that was the best thing Bart, who had recently found an occasional gray hair on his head, could say about the passage of time: *it healed.* For the kind of thing that had happened to the boy, there was nothing else to soften the hurt and diminish the bewilderment.

Jim was a good boy — a smart, quick, and perceptive one, as he had proved at the wood-cutters' camp. And a troubled one, as he had also proved. Bart had thought about their taking him in. He had been wary at first, but not later. He drained the glass and put it behind him on the mantle. He was worrying, too. He did not want anything to happen up there on Wild Horse Mesa that would cause more grief.

Hell, lightning strikes were always starting fires in the mountains, or maybe it was raining as hard up there as it was down here, in which case the fires wouldn't be able to burn. They did for a fact strike people now and then, but that was a huge country up there, and Jim was one small person. The odds of him being anywhere near where the bolt struck must be astronomical.

He turned and said, "What do you want me to do?"

Nan's very dark eyes softened as she welcomed the question, but she was not often impractical, and not impractical at all with the everyday tribulations and tests of life. "There is nothing we can do. Not right now. Maybe, if it passes by morning . . ."

He was gently wagging his head. "Not this

one, Sweetheart. We'll be lucky if it slacks up by day after tomorrow."

Even as she had suggested that the storm might pass, she had known in her heart it wouldn't. Not this kind of storm. She had grown up in this country; she knew about storms.

"When it does, we could pack a horse and ride up there."

He nodded mechanically because he had known this was coming. Riding thirty miles through mud and shallow lakes in unlikely places where the earth, unable to absorb more water, held it on the surface in mile-wide stretches, would be hard going. And if the sun came out hot as it commonly did in summertime after a thunderstorm, it would be humidly hot and physically draining to ride beneath it as far as Wild Horse Mesa.

"Bart. . . ?"

He smiled at her. "Sure. Just as soon as we can."

She kissed his cheek and took his empty glass to the kitchen to be refilled, but when she poured a glassful for him it was more than two-thirds water and it was less than one-third whiskey.

In the morning she arose first and had the cook stove popping when he came through for his hat on the back of the door before going down to do the chores. It was still coming down. From the veranda it did not seem to him to have slackened off at all.

The corralled horses resembled drowned rats. They were anxious to be fed. There was no sign of Big Ben and his herd, but if any creatures on the range had weathered it since last night, it would be his loose stock. They might be domesticated, but they still had wild horse instincts when it came to seeking shelter, or fleeing from danger, or pawing through snow for feed.

He leaned on the fork, looking at the unbroken expanse of grey and black which seemed to reach from one horizon to the other one. There were pools forming in the yard and elsewhere. After this storm passed, people would be contradicting each other and arguing for years about just how much water come down in one twenty-four hour period. They were still doing that about storms they had survived five, ten, maybe even fifty years earlier.

He grunted, draped the fork between its wooden pegs, and went sloshing back toward the house to be fed.

There was damned little people could do in this kind of weather, except perhaps patch harness, renail corral boards, take the sag out of gates, and maybe shoe horses, but that was an unpleasant job when horse's feet were soaked, caked with mud and too slippery to hold.

He turned just before entering the house for a final look northward. A sliver of pewter light showed through a slit in the undercast. Up north anyway, the storm was weakening. When he entered the kitchen, Nan raised her eyes to him as he draped his water-darkened old hat from the peg on the door. He smiled at her. "Maybe tomorrow. If it's goin' to slack off, we'd ought to see some sign of it by this evening."

It occurred before that.

CHAPTER 17
RETURN OF THE SUN

Even early in the summer, when the air was scrubbed clean and the sun broke through an undercast, the wet earth steamed and burned hotly against rooftops. By midsummer the effect was the same, only hotter.

Bart was down at the barn, fuming over a whittled elm handle that would not fit into the thin steel collar of the pitchfork he had whittled it for, and Nan was cleaning house with an impatient woman's fury when the world was abruptly drowned in pale golden brilliance. It was so starkly dazzling, it hurt the eyes.

Within fifteen minutes steam was rising. The puddles did not diminish, or if they did after an hour or two of that intense warmth, it was not noticeable.

Nan hurried to the barn where Bart had finally whittled enough of a slope to force the new handle onto the old fork, and said, "I'm going to make us something to eat."

He looked up. "Nan, we had dinner not an hour ago."

"Not to eat now," she explained, "to take with us." She whirled and was gone before he could hang the fork between its pegs and face her.

He moved to the doorless front barn opening, tipped back his head and squinted, but very briefly because the sunshine was fierce. Whatever had triggered the passing of the storm must have been very powerful. There were shreds of dispersing storm clouds to the west as well as to the south, no longer connected and no longer threatening.

Visibility was excellent, as it usually was after a heavy downpour. He could see the barranca so clearly it looked to be no more than five miles distant, and as he stood gazing at it, he wished to hell it was no farther than that.

He went out back to bring the horses in to be saddled. It required time and four croaker sacks to get their backs dry enough. He worked without really thinking, but his mood was less than exhilarated. The boy was all right. They were going to bust their buttons getting up there, and he was going to be hunkering at a fire looking annoyed and resentful. If she was like this before they'd even had the lad around for a while, what would she be like later? Or maybe if they had a child of their own? There was more than one side to a woman.

When he was finishing up, waiting for the animals to lip up the last of their rolled barley, she arrived carrying his shell belt and booted carbine, his old coat and blanketroll, so he would not have to waste time going to the house, and back.

He put the things she had brought into their saddlebags, distributing them evenly, and when she had watched him for a moment or two, moved over and kissed him, he smiled at her, indulgently, but also fondly. It was her nature to be a mother hen, and he certainly had not objected last year when a horse had thrown him against a gate post and nearly wrecked him, and she had ridden over to nurse and care for him.

They left the yard with heat on their backs and mud down below. But rising steam meant the ground was drying. With this kind of sunlight it would dry fast. Providing the sunlight lasted a week or so. He squinted at the sky. It was flawless. Even those distant clouds were gone.

Nan said, "We can make it up to the Wilton's camp by nightfall, can't we?"

He thought they could. "Maybe," he replied, then waved his arm to indicate the dozens of shallow pools, some nearly as large as small lakes. "But we can't make very good time."

They did, though, because they only paused twice and those times were to rest the animals, neither of which really needed much rest. They were both ridden down to tough, muscular condition.

They saw a drowned coyote and farther along, a cougar who had no business being down out of his mountains, except that cows calved in springtime, some early, some late, and cougars, like coyotes, throve on afterbirth. The big cats also killed calves, but Bart watched the cougar trying to get far from the oncoming riders and stopping each time it emerged from one of those pools to lift each foot separately and shake it, the way house cats did, and never once reached for the carbine under his leg.

The birds huddled disconsolately. For once they did not raise a ruckus when horsemen passed by. The deer, on the other hand, were along the creek and elsewhere, in thickets of tough underbrush, browsing as though there had been no storm.

The heat bore down. Bart shed his coat and shook his head. There was shade, but scattered and infrequent, none of it on the trail they were riding.

Nan smiled each time he looked in her direction. Once, she said, "I think he'll be glad to see us."

Bart doubted it, so he changed the subject. "Supposing he comes back with us; where do we put him?"

She gave him a very grave look. "Bart, you don't really want him, do you?"

His brows dropped a notch. "Nan — "

"Tell me the truth."

He looked steadily at her. "I'll tell you the truth. I'll always tell you the truth. Yes, I want him to come back with us. But I'm not sure he'll want to, and it makes me uncomfortable to see you building up a lot of hope."

She smiled a little. "If he doesn't want to, it won't be the first disappointment I've ever had. But he needs us. More than he realizes."

"Yeah," he agreed dryly. "That's my point, sweetheart. More than he realizes."

She rode a while in thoughtful silence, then spoke again. "We could build a room onto the house, couldn't we?"

He wanted to throw up his hands. Instead he nodded his head. "Sure. And he'd learn something about draw-knifing logs, notching them, and chinking the places where they don't fit real good."

She was pleased. "You see, you think about him as someone you can teach things to. Like a son."

He wanted to laugh. For her sake, he hoped very hard Jim would be persuaded to come back with them. Something else also occurred to him: he liked the boy very much, but if he hadn't, he would have yielded to her because he wanted her to be happy. That, he told himself emphatically, was something else he had just learned about being married.

In a part of the country that was normally without mosquitoes, they came out of nowhere in the dazzling, humid heat to bother riders and horses. It reminded him of the low place where those horse thieves had put up a battle.

The sun was leaving. It did not turn rusty red as it usually did this time of year as it went down, and the heat remained. They had crossed two little creeks, swollen now to nearly river-size, and were heading more east than north in the direction of that old military road, which was also in the direction of the Wilton's wagon-camp.

He had not thought about little Emily with her baby and long-legged, rawboned Emory up to this point, except to speculate about being able to reach their camp before full dark. They must have caught hell last night. The best waterproof wagon-canvas usually leaked where it rubbed against the bows, or at the corners where the grommets held tiedown ropes.

They saw smoke rising above treetops long

before they saw the wagon, which meant that whatever the emigrants had gone through last night they had survived it. Later, with dusk spreading, they rode through the timber and smelled not just the wood-smoke but also food cooking.

As they came forth into the little open place where the forlorn old wagon stood, tongue kept off the ground by a round of firewood, they saw Emory batting at smoke with an old hat while reaching the full length of his long arms to stir stew with a wooden ladle. He was too preoccupied to notice them until Bart whistled; then he stood up to wipe his eyes on a soiled cuff.

Emily was in the wagon. She came down over the tailgate as nimble as a squirrel, and smiled broadly as she came forward, automatically drying her hands on her apron, although they had not been wet.

After the greetings Emily took Nan to the wagon where the baby was bone-dry and wrapped like a cocoon. She told Nan that because they'd been unable to make more than two or three diapers out of the cloth they could spare to cut up, she had borrowed a custom from the Indians; she used tree moss, and it worked very well.

Emory remained out with Bart until the horses had been hobbled and turned loose.

When Bart asked how they had weathered the storm, Emory answered confidently. "We been waitin' for the ground to set up so's I could put in a garden patch, an' meanwhile we been blazin' trees for cabin logs, an' yesterday with everything ready, saws sharp and all, I saw that storm coming when I got out of bed in the morning, so I had all day to take down the canvas, spread it, mix the coal oil and melt the wax and paint it on. Barely got it back over the bows in the late afternoon before the first raindrops come." He beamed. "We stayed as dry as ticks in a shaggy rug."

They strolled back to the fire. On the way Bart explained about Jim and why they were heading up through this area. Emory looked at him and said, "They have a hard lot, don't they?" Bart nodded while letting his gaze wander around the crude, primitive wagon-camp as Emory continued, "But seems to me they brought most of it on themselves, killin' women an' children, burning folks out, lifting hair and all."

Bart considered the stew in its big old iron pot. There was enough to feed a small army. Hunting must have been good for Emory lately. He said, "Yeah, they brought a lot of it on themselves, but we helped them get into the mood for it. I've never been able to make up my mind about who was wrong and who was right. Mostly, that's a waste of time; the wars are past. Now, seems the thing to do is help those that want help and ask for it. The rest," Bart looked up at the taller man and smiled, "let them keep the blanket."

Emory Wilton said that one of the Holbrook riders had returned his horses yesterday, leading them behind the tailgate of a light wagon. He had also left six sacks of seed grain Mr. Holbrook had sent along. He was pleased and gestured down toward open country. "I made a sod-buster out of a red fir log, drove harrow spikes through it three inches apart. It's not a plow, but I think it'll work. Maybe I'll have to criss-cross the land four or five times to break up the sod and uproot the native grass, but I got the time." He dropped his arm. "With that much grain, a man could harvest more than enough to see him through."

Emily and Nan returned. Nan was carrying the baby. Bart thought it looked as fat as a shoat. Mother's milk, maybe like doe-deer milk, was twice as rich as cow's milk.

It was a healthy, strong child. When Nan came over and Bart put his hand down, the baby gripped one finger with surprising strength.

Later, with darkness hovering less than fifty feet from the firelighted small clearing, back where the timber made a thick screen, Emory spoke meanderingly of his plans for the future, while his wife rocked the sleeping baby in her arms and gazed at her husband with absolute confidence. Once, she asked about Dr. Mailer, the practising physician down in Holtville who had delivered her baby under peculiar circumstances last year. She considered Frank Mailer very close to being a saint.

It was a comfortable time, pleasant, warm, and relaxed. So relaxed that Bart was fighting off sleep for an hour before he and Nan declined an offer to sleep in the wagon, took their bedrolls among the trees to dry ground, and rolled in.

There were bright stars by the thousands, not twinkling as they ordinarily did, just hanging up there glowing. Nan groped for his hand and held it without pressure. He was almost asleep when she said, "I'm glad it worked out for them."

His reply was a grunt.

She raised her head, watched him for a moment, sank back down still holding his work callused hand and looked straight up. Love was a peculiar emotion. She continued to gaze at the stars as though they might offer an enlightening explanation to this, until she fell asleep.

They did not wait for breakfast in the morning. This close to the high plateau, Bart was anxious to be in the saddle.

As they rode through a dense stand of thornpin and emerged in an area of pine stumps and flourishing second growth, he saw the old road. He looked back as he said, "Two hours more."

It was an optimistic guess; the storm had deepened the washouts and had created new ones. As they were picking their way around a particularly deep one, Bart reflected on what might have been the case if Nan's father had not brought a team up here to take Alex, Foster, and Abel down with their laden wagon. With the condition the old road was in now, they could not have made it in a wagon. Not even an empty one. From now on, anyone going up to the big meadow would have to ride horseback.

In fact, unless someone took the time to come up here and chuck rocks into the worst of the gullies, it would even become hazardous on horseback, if there was another storm like that one night before last.

He was still thinking about this, from the standpoint of a wild horse trapper, when Nan said she smelled smoke.

He smelled it too when they were about midway. "Lightning strike," he said, and did not add that it must have been a particularly bad lightning strike to start a fire that had burned through that downpour and seemed to still be burning.

They came up over the last pitch in the trail and rode out upon the immense grassland plateau with the sun barely clearing the topmost treetops northward, when they saw the smoke. It was not rising fast nor spreading the way smoke rose from fiercely burning wood below it. This smoke was drifting slowly as though it had been created by coals in a old deadfall log, perhaps saturated with water; otherwise, the smoke would not have been as thick and soiled-looking.

They rode across the huge meadow side by side, silent and apprehensive. Not because of the smoke but because of a shared feeling neither of them could explain.

The sun was high before they got completely across and close to the timber. Where they halted was midway between Bart's wild horse corrals and the more easterly site where Abel, Alex, and Foster'd had their wood camp.

There was absolute silence. The only moving thing they saw was that lazy spindrift of rising smoke. It appeared to be slightly to their left and northward.

Nan asked where Jim'd had his camp. Bart

could not answer because he had never asked the lad, and Jim had never volunteered this information. He thought the camp was northwest, but he did not mention this because that was the direction of the rising smoke.

They entered the forest over soggy fir needles where the fragrance was very strong of tree sap and rotting needles. The heat would reach the meadow behind them but not up where they were riding because sunlight pierced the treetops only in a few places.

Bart stopped abruptly with an upraised gloved hand. His wife drew rein behind him. There was a horse cropping grass in a little clearing where sunlight reached. The animal had not seen them. It was thoroughly enjoying the increasing heat after what it had gone through last night. It was also enjoying being able to selectively pick grass heads, something it was not often able to do on the lower range.

When Bart said he recognized the animal, the horse threw up its head at the sound of a human voice and froze. Nan also knew the horse. "The camp can't be far," she said.

It wasn't far. Neither was a wide area of black scorch. To one side lay the huge old rotting deadfall from which the smoke was rising. It was smouldering deep in its heart where the wood was still hard, red, and flammable, but water had so thoroughly soaked in that a flaming fire would not break out although the log could smoulder for weeks.

They knew it was a human camp because of the bridle hanging from a tree limb, and the other things, mostly hand-crafted, lying in the trampled grass.

They dismounted and while Bart walked carefully through the grass and weeds to the left, Nan was doing the same to their right. The smell of sulphur was strong even now, almost two days after the lightning had struck.

Nan probably realized it without Bart commenting; what she had seen from thirty miles distant and had been impressed with because it had been an unusually massive and blinding flash, had clearly been one of the most violent strikes of lightning either of them would ever experience, and where they were walking the stench of scorched wood was even stronger than the other smell, the sulphur scent which was a residue of such a mighty electrical charge that tree trunks had been charred by it as far off as two hundred and fifty feet.

CHAPTER 18
ANOTHER DAY

They searched hard but found no trace of Jim Moore. When they came together beneath the tree holding the bridle, Bart raised his hat to scratch. "Hell of a poor place to camp anyway," he said, looking around. "There's no shelter, he'd be exposed if it rained or if a big wind came." He looked puzzled, with justification. Nan's reaction to failure was more emotional than practical.

"Wouldn't there be something?" She gestured. "If he had been out here when it struck, wouldn't there be — something?"

He did not want to say what he thought: if Jim had been out here, he would probably have been incinerated.

She was pale. "Burnt clothing, something . . ."

To get her mind off the worst of the possibilities, he suggested widening the scope of their search. They got back astride and reined off in different directions. Beyond the scorched trees, there was rough country,

236

some of it piled with lava-like jumbles of rock, some of it twisted and up-ended with deep arroyos and narrow gullies choked with underbrush.

As Bart rode along the rocky rim of a deep place he thought that this would be ideal bear-hunting country. It had most of the things bears liked, including flourishing bushes of mountain berries down the slopes and scarcely-heard little creeks of run-off water from those perpetually snow-clad higher northward peaks.

If a bear had got the boy, it was unlikely that there would be clothing out where they had searched on foot. Bears commonly picked up their victims and carried them to some particular place before eating them.

He dismounted beside a craggy, high plinth of rough dark rock, climbed it, and was disappointed that the view from the top let him see nothing but more miles of timber in all directions. Timber, scatterings of more huge rocks, and little else.

He rode away from this place more concerned with finding his wife than Jim Moore. He continued to search as the sun climbed, and turned back toward the place where they had parted only when the sun began moving downward in a westerly direction. They had spent most of the day searching. At this elevation, it got very cold during the night. They had some food and their bedrolls, but they would also need a fire and plenty of wood to feed it if they spent the night up here. They would have to gather the wood before dusk.

When he got back to the burned tree where the bridle was hanging, he dismounted, hobbled his horse, lifted off the outfit, and went after armloads of dry limbs. By the time he had enough firewood to last the night, dusk was approaching. He killed more time by making a small fire, which burned with an intense blue flame and no smoke. He finally stood up and called. Nan should be within hearing, and it was getting too dark to search. If she had not already started back, his call would probably encourage her to.

But she did not arrive.

He worried and called several more times. She still did not ride toward his little fire from the timber. As his fear mounted and daylight continued to wane, he went to his saddle, freed the old riding coat from behind the cantle, shrugged into it, took his Winchester, and went on foot in the direction Nan had taken.

It was too late to track her. Even in broad daylight, it would not have been easy to track her where there were only layers of fir needles, although it should have been marginally easier after the storm had soaked everything.

He called several times as he hunted, stopping often to listen. He was more than worried by now; he was very much afraid. She would have answered if she had heard him. There was always danger in this kind of country, just riding along a narrow ridge above a deep crevice, for example, if the ground underfoot became slick granite, and something spooked her horse. Some of those gullys were very deep.

He blamed himself for not riding with her, for although this would have made the search longer, at least he would have been with her if something had happened.

He was approaching one of those jumbles of blackish rock when a startled cow elk that had been meandering southward, came around the rocks and saw the man with the gun directly in front of her. She turned to stone. They eyed each other. Bart was not the least bit interested in the cow elk. He sat on a waist-high moss-mottled rock and looked at her. She looked back, and continued to do so until Bart tilted his head and yelled his wife's name again. That made the elk wheel like a reined saddlehorse and go plunging blindly through the darkening forest.

She made so much noise Bart barely heard what he thought might be a human shout. He stood up gripping the Winchester and waited for the shout, if it had indeed been a human cry, to be repeated. The cow elk passed from sight, and eventually also from hearing, and for as long as Bart stood waiting the only sound he heard was a faint high breeze in the treetops.

But it had come from the southwest. He was certain of that, so he turned slightly down-slope, bearing westward as he walked.

He halted in near darkness, listened, then threw back his head and called her name again. This time as he was preparing to continue walking, the call came distinctly.

"Bart! I found him!"

He made a slight change in his course and took longer strides. When he was uncertain he called, and she answered him. By this method he was able to walk toward a pile of very large rocks, some as big as a horse.

He was almost certain this was where her voice had come from, and his judgment was confirmed when he saw her flashy chestnut horse standing tethered to the lowest limb of an old fir tree, looking thoroughly bored.

The last time he called, he did not raise his voice very much. When the answer came back, it startled him. It seemed to come from directly below his feet.

In front to his right, where the foremost boulders were strewn and stacked, there was what appeared to be a bear den, an old one, probably long abandoned. Even the scattering of crushed bones were bleached white. He approached it, dropped to one knee to peer in, and detected the scent of stale damp air. He said, "Nan?"

Her reply was in a normal tone. "In here. Watch your head."

He got down on all fours. For about fifteen feet it was a tight fit. Beyond that the cave became wider and high, not high enough for a man to stand erect, but high enough for him to stand up bent over.

Nan's face showed eerily in what little light there was. When she saw him, she stood up in a crouch and gestured for him to go back the way he had come. He could see nothing behind her, partly because her body blocked his sight, partly because of the darkness. He turned and went back out the crawl-hole, stood up to one side, and as she emerged, reached to help her.

"How in hell did you find that cave?" he asked. She ignored the question. She had something much more important on her mind. She looked steadily at him and spoke in almost a whisper.

"He's blind."

Bart was prepared for almost anything but this. A broken leg, perhaps — or a fever — maybe even injuries sustained from being attacked by a large animal. He gazed blankly at her. "Blind?"

"Yes. I was riding through here. He called. It sounded like a puppy. He's huddled in there like an injured animal. I gave him water from my canteen. He drank half of it. But when I went after some food in my saddle-bags, he wouldn't eat. He's been in there . . . he told me he was returning from that glade about a mile south where he left the horse when the lightning struck. It lifted him in the air. He remembers that but nothing else, except that when he came to, his side hurt where he had evidently been slammed against a tree."

"Broken ribs?"

"No. I felt for that. He couldn't see and it was raining hard. He knew where this cave was because that's where he slept at night when he lived up here before. Bart, he crawled on his hands and knees to hole up in there. He told me he thought he was going to die — was waiting to die — when he heard my horse. He thought it was the animal he'd come up here on, so he talked to it."

Bart looked for something to sit on. There was nothing so he leaned on a bug-tree that was already dying at the top and losing needles. "Plumb blind? Can't see at all?"

"Yes."

He groped for a straw as he said, "It's dark in there, Nan. Maybe that's it. He hasn't come out so he don't think he can — ."

"Bart, he is blind."

He accepted that without further comment, continued to lean for a moment, then straightened up. "Well, we can get him out of there; put him behind you on the horse and take him back to camp."

That is what they did, not without difficulty because the boy was not willing. He had a fatalistic temperament, like many Indians Bart had heard about. He'd had two days to decide it was his time to die, and the idea was solidly fixed in his mind. He was resigned to dying. They had to talk hard to convince him that if it had indeed been his time, then why did his private star send Nan riding to the cave?

He was weak, and his clothes, including the ragged old sweater, had that peculiar sulphur scent and were torn. But when they reached Bart's little fire and had fed it up into a bright blaze, they could find no sign of burns. A couple of bruises but no burns, which Bart thought was in itself a miracle. He must have been very close to the strike to be flung off his feet by it. The trees a couple of hundred feet distant had been seared.

Nan made a meal. Jim did not seem to want to talk, so Bart abandoned the effort until they were all warm and fed. He was refilling the lad's cup with coffee, when he began to ask questions, and the words tumbled out. Bart and Nan exchanged a glance. The shock of being knocked unconscious by a lightning strike was enough to make anyone reticent, but being unable to see afterwards would be far worse. It would drive most people into shocked silence, and pure terror, for at least days.

But Jim retold his experience, speaking slowly and adding details he'd neglected to mention to Nan, and several times he raised a palm to pass it in front of his eyes because, although he could hear the bright fire burning and crackling and could feel its heat, he could not see it.

By the time they were ready to bed down, Nan's initial shock had passed. By firelight Bart could see her brimming tears. They made Jim comfortable beside the fire, wrapping him in two blankets, one each from their individual blanketrolls, then they walked out a short ways and Nan said, "I can't remember ever having anything hurt me like this. I could bawl."

He turned her by the shoulders. "All right, bawl."

"No. Maybe later, when I'm able to hide it in the blankets. . . . Blind? Sixteen years old, and so blind he can't even see the fire?"

Bart had nothing to say. During his lifetime he had occasionally indulged, as all rangemen did at one time or another, in thoughts of personal injury. Working the ranges was a dangerous occupation. Anyone who continued to do it eventually received at least one bad injury. But not blindness. He had considered an entire range of things that could happen to him before he quit, and not once had blindness been one of them.

A man could get by without a leg. He'd seen men do it. Even without an arm. Or with disintegrating spines, or frozen fingers and toes. Broken bones that ultimately healed went with the occupation. But a blind man couldn't even see the floor to find his boots, or find his chin to shave it, or — hell!

He kissed his wife's cheek. "We'll head down at sunrise and go directly home with him."

She shook her head. "I'll take him home. You ride to Holtville and bring back Dr. Mailer."

He nodded and held back his thoughts. What good could a doctor or anyone else do when someone was blind? Nothing. Every town of any size had blind people in it. If there were a cure for blindness, they had never heard of it, and for a damned fact no blind man would ever stop seeking and asking.

He turned toward the fire when she stopped him with a hand on his arm. "Bart, I can't do this to you."

"Do what?"

"We wanted to take him in, to raise him . . ."

He looked hard at her. "He didn't do that on purpose. It wasn't his fault, an' he's still a kid, a damned badly scairt one right now, I'd say, without a single human being on earth to hold out a hand to him. We're going to take him back, an' if we got to tie ropes from the house to the barn to the springhouse, we'll do it."

She threw her arms around him briefly, then walked back with him. Nothing more was said until morning when he walked through heavy dew to bring in the horses, and because it was a longer walk down to the little glade where Jim's horse was, by the time they had eaten and were ready to head down to open country, the sun was high.

Nan led Jim's horse, and Bart picked a different trail down, one wide enough for two horses abreast to pass without interference from big trees.

Jim knew when they were out of the timber. He could feel the heat. He had been especially quiet since last night. The Templetons let things go like that until they were two-thirds of the way home, well past the creek where they had met him, quite a few miles southwest of the Wilton's wagon-camp, and making good time because although the ground underfoot was muddy, most of that ground water was gone. They could ride in a straight line. Bart wanted to reach the yard before midnight so he said nothing about making a night camp. Nan did not mention her earlier suggestion that he head for town for an excellent reason; her husband clearly did not intend to leave her riding through the night with the blind youth.

The horses were tired, so were their riders, and finally Jim offered to talk. He mentioned his fear while hiding in the cave. He knew, because he now had fleas, that the cave had once been a bear den. And although the smell was not strong, which meant no bears had used the cave in a long while, it was always possible that a bear might seek the cave during a bad storm, or later, when the storm had passed and one might decide to den up until it was dry, or perhaps to drag in a deer carcass to eat undisturbed.

Bart and Nan exchanged a glance during this recital. Bad enough to be unable to see, but to live in dread of an encounter with a bear inside a cave where he would not have been able to escape, must have made Jim's terror very great.

Then he smiled and said, "I was going to come back. I was going to start down this morning and return the horse." He groped through ragged pockets and produced Nan's belt. "And bring this to you." He pushed the belt toward where he had been listening to her voice. She took it and thanked him with a lump in her throat the size of a rock.

He looked ahead where he could distinguish the separate sound of Bart's horse up ahead. It required a little time for him to say it, but he tried. "I could go back to my cave. I might even be able to find the reservation again. But now I don't have anyone."

Nan reined close and leaned with an arm around his shoulders in a protective way. "Will you do us a favor, Jim?"

He replied without hesitation. "Yes'm."

"Will you live with us?"

Bart was riding twisted in the saddle. He saw the lad's mouth quiver and reined back to ride upon his opposite side as he said, "Jim, we can build a lean-to bedroom and you can — "

The words were torn out of him very loud. "I can't see! I'm blind! I — couldn't even find the lean-to! If I go back to the cave, I can sit in there and wait."

Bart met his wife's swimming eyes over the boy's head and cleared his throat to rid it of the tight, slightly burning sensation, then he spoke loudly. "You can do just about anything you set your mind to do, Jim, and we'll help you do it. Boy, eyes aren't everything. Suppose you'd lost both your legs. Or maybe busted your back so's you'd have to spend the rest of your life sittin' in a chair without being able to move. Listen to me; we need you with us. You've got a family and families work together for one another. Now smile at me, boy. *Smile!*"

It was a wet-eyed, quavery smile but it rose to his face and when Bart leaned to take his hand, and squeezed, Jim squeezed back.

CHAPTER 19
A TIME OF TRIAL

Nan cooked a meal. The house was warm, and Jim sat in the parlor as motionless as a large rag doll until Bart was kneeling at the hearth to build a fire and said, "Darn good thing you weren't closer when that bolt struck."

The lad said nothing. His expression suggested, though, that he wished he had been closer, so there would be no blindness.

Bart fed in the kindling, lighted it, rocked back for a moment, then eased in two large quarters of a red fir round. The fire briefly faded before flaring brilliantly.

It was very late, later than Bart had been up and around in years. When Nan called them to the kitchen, Bart did not take Jim's hand; he put an arm around the youth's shoulders and guided him that way, while talking about the storm without mentioning the lightning.

Jim's depression did not go as deep as his hunger. After Nan and Bart had finished and were sipping coffee, the young Indian went right on scarfing up just about everything he could eat.

Bart went down to the barn to look in on the animals. Nan made a bed on the sofa near the hearth for Jim. He was drowsy; it was hotter in the house than he was accustomed to, and he had eaten as much as a much larger man. He was also emotionally exhausted whether he would allow it to show or not. Nan made him comfortable, turned down the lamp without remembering that it would not keep him awake, then left the house on her way to the barn.

Her husband was rigging out a fresh horse. When she appeared, he spoke before she could. "It's a long ride. Twice as long as it was up to Wild Horse Mesa, so I better leave right now."

"But you haven't rested, Bart."

He grinned at her in the gloom. "We're tough. Jim an' I are tough. We trotted most of the way from the mesa to Wilton's camp, remember, then rode darned near another twenty miles southward after those horse thieves, and we hadn't had much rest than either." He dropped the stirrup, shoved the tag-end of the latigo through its little holder, and turned to lead the horse out of the barn. Nan followed, and said, "I don't like you doing this, Bart. I wish there was another way." She suddenly brightened. "You could ride over and waken my father. He'd send one of the riders and you could rest."

He trailed the reins to get close enough to kiss her, smiled, and turned back to swing into the saddle. From there, still tenderly smiling, he said, "Take care of yourself."

She watched him cross the yard and fade into the darkness. When she could no longer hear him, she went wearily back to the house, set the damper on the kitchen stove, banked the hearth fire, stood a long time looking down at the sleeping youth, then went off to bed.

She had been tired before, many times, but never as tired as she was tonight as she got ready for bed. Her weariness this time seemed more of the spirit than of the body.

In the morning when she passed through the parlor on the way to the kitchen, she glanced at the couch. It was empty. With a sinking feeling, she hurried to the front veranda. He was not in sight. She ran down to the barn. He was not there either, so she went out back and counted the horses. They were all in the corral.

She returned to the house as Jim came in from out back where he'd groped his way to the wash house. She could have dropped she was so relieved, but instead she went over to

252

help him find the kitchen door. As he sat at the table, she talked, he listened, and when the meal was ready, so was he. Again, she was astonished at how much food he could put away.

Later, she walked with him hand-in-hand down to the barn. He asked about her husband. She told him where he had gone, and Jim turned his face toward the sound of her voice. "Medicine won't make new eyes," he said.

She had to answer encouragingly, so she said, "We don't know what medicine can do. We won't know until Dr. Mailer gets here. Maybe tomorrow." She released his hand as they entered the shadowy, cool barn. "He is a fine doctor." She told him what Dr. Mailer had done for her father last year, as well as for the emigrant's wife. He had saved her life.

He felt his way along the saddle-pole to the stall-fronts on his way out back where Nan was going. He used her voice as his beacon. She watched his groping progress with approval — and an abiding pain.

The sun was climbing, the mud was firming up into the consistency of putty, and the horses nickered because they had not been fed, so Nan left Jim out there and went back for forksful of hay, which she pitched with an experienced toss.

Jim leaned on the peeled-pole stringers. "What does your husband do with all his horses?" he asked.

"Breaks them to sell when they are old enough."

"Doesn't he trap the wild ones, too?"

"Yes, but we have a fairly large herd of brood mares of our own. He goes up there to trap wild horses because he likes to do it."

"Where are Alex and Foster and Abel?"

"They've gone back to town with their wood. If you'd like, one of these days we'll ride in and visit them. Would you like that?"

"Yes." Then he hesitated and said, "What will they do with my brothers?"

She was leaning on the hayfork watching his face. It kept her alert, trying to keep track of his abrupt changes in their conversation. She said, "Probably bury them in the Holtville cemetary."

He looked in the direction of her voice. "Indians?"

She understood. Maybe they would not be buried there. Her father had once snorted over something like this. He had told her as far as he could see, it did not make any difference who was planted in a cemetery; it only mattered to living people that dead Indians, or Mexicans, or anyone people did not want buried among their departed friends and families should be excluded. He had said, "I'd risk a guess that the folks buried in any cemetery got a lot more in common with each other than they have with whoever they left behind. Seems to me about the only way folks become plumb equal is to lie together in a graveyard."

She got around the problem by saying it might be better if his brothers were buried over in her family cemetery. Jim had a different idea. "Couldn't they be buried here? I could memorize how many steps it was out to their graves."

She replied before she thought. "Yes." Then it struck her that this time of year his brothers had probably already been buried because early burials were mandatory in this heat. But she did not mention any of this. She instead took him back through the barn with her to the yard, and on across to the house.

While she worked in the kitchen, he sat at the table following her movements by sound. Later, he startled her by announcing that someone was driving into the yard in a buggy. She went out front and met her father who was already tying up in front of the barn. He waved to her, then squinted in the direction of the corrals. He had recognized the horse the Indian lad had ridden away on.

Nan came down to him and before he could ask questions, told him everything that had happened since the night of the storm. His reaction to Jim's condition was identical to Bart's reaction. He stared at her. "Blind? Can't see?"

"Can't see," she repeated.

John Holbrook leaned on the hitchrack, gazing at her. She made a quavery little forlorn smile. "Bart's gone to town for Dr. Mailer."

Holbrook continued to gaze at her. "Blind. . . . What can anyone do about that?"

She did not know, but she was unwilling to believe nothing could be done about it. "He worked a miracle for you last year."

Her father made a gesture. "Honey, it's not the same. I had that little bird arrow in my back. He removed it. Blind — blind is when your eyes just plain can't see."

He saw as soon as he had made that statement that she was barely holding onto her emotions. He straightened up off the hitchrack and said, "Well now, we'll just have to see about this, won't we? Maybe Frank Mailer knows about some doctors — maybe back east — who treat blindness. Don't you worry. We'll haul that kid all around the country until we find someone who can fix him."

She had her lower lip between her teeth and released it to smile again at her father, whom she now saw as a blurry vision facing her. She said, "Would you like something to eat? I was just making dinner when Jim heard your rig."

They went to the house. When they entered, Jim cocked his head and said, "It is your father."

John and his daughter looked at each other.

"He smelled the same way over in his yard before we went after the horse thieves. He smelled of whiskey and tobacco."

John laughed, pulled up a chair as his daughter went out to the kitchen, and leaned to tap Jim on the knee as he spoke. "If there's a blessed way to fix your eyes, we're goin' to find it."

Jim said nothing.

The older man straightened back in the chair, looking gravely at the youngster. He was not an individual given to pity, but neither was he an individual with a stone heart. "I once knew a man who couldn't see. He lost his sight in the war. He was so good at gettin' around and doing his work it was two weeks before I realized he was blind."

Jim remained expressionless and silent.

Holbrook squirmed on the chair, cast a look over his shoulder in the direction of the kitchen, then rapped Jim on the knee again, arose and went out to the kitchen. He and his daughter exchanged a look. John Holbrook wagged his head without saying a word.

He did not leave until late in the afternoon, and the last thing he told the young Indian, just before he picked up his hat on the way toward the door, was: "Don't give up, son. Don't just accept this. I expect it'll be a long fight, but you got to keep your heart strong. I know what I'm talkin' about. I was in pain more years than you are old before Dr. Mailer came along and fixed my back."

It was a brave little speech, and the older man had meant every word of it, but as he and his daughter strolled in the direction of the barn, his tone of voice was different. "How old is he?"

"Sixteen."

"Gawddamn, Nan, that's awful young to be blind."

"Yes. We'll keep him. He doesn't have anyone else. His brothers are dead, his parents are dead."

John Holbrook looked closely at his daughter. "Pity don't stand up as long as this thing may last."

"It's not pity," she replied. "We wanted to have him before this happened."

Holbrook freed his buggy horse and backed the rig clear of the rail so that when he climbed in the horse would be able to turn completely around. He blew out a big breath.

258

"Hell," he said. "I drove over to see how you two rode out that storm and maybe a little family talk." He climbed into the rig, which sagged under his weight. He evened up the lines but let them hang slack as he looked at her. "You're sure gettin' you share of miseries."

She smiled.

He smiled back. "You're tough. You always were. Think you three can come over Sunday?"

She was not sure, so they had to leave it at that, and as her father turned for the drive back, she watched the buggy, feeling sorry for him. The "miseries" she had experienced up until now were nothing compared to what he had gone through during his long lifetime.

She returned to the house, and Jim's face came around when the door opened and closed. His mood was different; her father had given him hope. He said, "He don't have to help an Indian."

She pulled the chair that her father had been sitting in close, took both his hands in her hands, and said, "Listen to me, Jim. My mother was Indian. You're going to have to learn that off the reservation there isn't the same feeling. . . . Not entirely, anyway. I want you to start thinking of people as just — people."

He nodded. That would not be hard since he would be unable to see the color of their skins.

She reached to brush back his long hair. "Tell me about your mother. Was she tall?"

"About a head shorter than you. But my father was tall. And he was strong. He hunted a lot. He taught me to use a bow and arrow and to shoot his old rifle."

She encouraged him to recall his parents, but she avoided anything that had to do with his brothers. Their deaths were too close, still too vivid and violent. But he did not appear to want to talk about them.

He told her of his childhood, of the soldiers and missionaries who came to the reservation, of his life up until he decided to leave the reservation.

She was an attentive listener, occasionally asking questions. Then he asked her a question. "Did your father marry your mother off the reservation?"

"Jim, there were no reservations when my father and mother were married. She was a spokesman's daughter, so it cost my father a lot of horses. They were married twice, once at my mother's rancheria and again by a minister my father sent for."

He did not make a sound when she finished speaking. His head was cocked a little. She knew the gesture and arose to go quickly to the door. But it was not a horseman, nor was it two horsemen as she had hoped very hard it might be. It was Big Ben the remount stallion bringing his mares into the yard.

She watched with interest because although Big Ben showed no fear of the buildings or the man scent, his mares were more wary and the colts rolled their eyes, prepared to whirl and flee if the mares balked with fear. The colts had had very little contact with humans, and usually then it had only been at a distance. Their mothers knew about men, but they had been running free long enough to have lost most of their tolerance for human beings.

But Big Ben had a memory like an elephant. He was poking here and there looking for that rangy big wild stallion who had knocked him senseless last year, the big horse Bart had left in the corral before leaving for Holtville.

But the big horse was no longer a stallion, so when Ben finally located him and cake-walked toward the corral bowing his neck and whistling a challenge, the big horse inside the corral merely walked over until they could touch muzzles, then turned away.

Big Ben took that dismissal as an act of cowardice and came off the ground pawing at the corral stringers. His sudden, violent display startled the mares and colts. They spun and left the yard in a belly-down rush.

Nan went down toward the corrals searching in mud for stones as she walked. When she had a handful she got close enough to the thick-necked stallion to hit him hard several times before he stopped making challenges and turned to face her. She threw two more stones, high overhand. One missed by inches, but the second one struck Big Ben squarely in the middle of the back. He sprang ahead and sideways, making a loud snort.

Nan raised her arm with an empty hand and that was all the remount stallion needed to see. He went out of the yard flinging mud in all direction, tail out, head up and swinging from side to side.

Nan walked back to the veranda and stood in the failing daylight, watching the horses. Ben did not stop when he reached the band but swept up the side of them, got in the lead, and trumpeted for them to follow. They obeyed. Five minutes later they were out of sight.

Nan turned to peer westward, the direction from which her husband would arrive with the doctor. There was only empty space, miles and miles of it, and a sky turning burnished red-gold.

CHAPTER 20
DR. MAILER

The morning dragged. When her father had visited the previous day, she had been provided with a diversion from her pain and sadness. Today, even though the weather was softly warm, the sky flawless and the air as clear as glass, she could not shake off a feeling of depression.

At least, not until an hour before noon, when Jim told her someone was coming from the east. She had coaxed him to the veranda where he had been sitting when he called her, and as before, although he was facing that direction, she marveled at his ability to detect sounds at a distance. And he was right, two horsemen were loping toward the yard. One she recognised by the way he sat his saddle as her husband; the other man was thicker, heavier, and older. By the time Bart raised a hand to her in a high salute, she recognized Dr. Mailer.

She watched them enter the yard and disappear inside the barn. While she waited for them to emerge, she reached for a porch-upright and held it. Her knees were weak, for while she hoped very hard, she also had a faint but persevering dread.

Frank Mailer was a quiet, thoughtful man with the physique of a blacksmith. The first time she had seen him he had been wearing an ivory-handled Colt and had seemed unable to smile. His sentences had been clipped, direct and incisive. That was over a year ago. Today, as he approached the veranda with her husband, he was not wearing a weapon beneath his light coat, and he was carrying a small black leather satchel. Otherwise, he looked the same — slightly rumpled, darkly tanned, steady-eyed. But he smiled as he came up the steps and she greeted him. He glanced past her swiftly, then back again.

Bart mentioned something to eat, and Frank Mailer declined. They'd had breakfast on the trail, and for all his thick build he was not a big eater. But when Nan mentioned coffee, he trailed after her into the house, leaving Bart on the porch with Jim.

In the kitchen, as he put his satchel on the floor and sat at the table, he considered Nan for a while in silence, then cleared his throat and in his direct manner asked if there had been any improvement in the boy since her husband had left for town.

264

She brought him his coffee and shook her head. "None that I can tell and he doesn't say much."

Dr. Mailer was raising the cup when he said, "Indian," as though that explained the boy's reticence. The coffee was too hot so he blew on it. He did not look at her when he said, "Bart said the bolt lifted him and flung him against a tree."

Nan nodded. "That's what he told us."

Mailer continued to blow on the coffee. "Bart also said the lad was several hundred feet or more from where the bolt struck."

"Yes. I think that's what we figured the distance had to be."

"Burnt clothing, Nan?"

"His clothing smelled of sulphur, Frank, and some of it was torn."

His eyes came over the rim of the coffee cup. "Scorched, Nan?"

She thought back. He had looked so terribly injured and bedraggled, so disheveled. "I think so. . . . No, I don't remember seeing any signs of scorch." She sat down slowly, placed her arms atop the table, and gazed at the older man, who was now able to sip the coffee. She was hoping very hard.

As the doctor put down his cup, he brusquely said, "Well, we'd better fetch him in so I can have a look at him." She was arising when he asked another question. "For the last couple of days you've been with him?"

"Yes."

"Does he try to stay in the dark, or avoid sunlight?"

"No, not particularly, but then except for going down to the barn to do the chores, we've pretty much remained inside. I'll get him. Help yourself to more coffee, Frank."

He smiled, nodded his head absently and watched her cross the parlor toward the front door. He half-filled the crockery mug from the pot on the stove, and brought forth a pony of brandy, tipped some into the coffee, pocketed the small bottle and was standing with his back to the stove sipping when Nan, her husband, and Jim Moore entered the kitchen. The Templetons stood expectantly by the table. Jim felt for a chair back and held it as the bull-built man by the stove continued to sip coffee for a few moments, studying the youth.

When he put the cup aside, Dr. Mailer pulled out two chairs, pulled Jim toward one, and pushed him down. He took the other chair and leaned close as he said, "Jim, tell me everything you remember up on the mesa when the lightning struck. Everything. Don't leave anything out."

"I was coming back from putting the horse

I borrowed in a little grassy place, maybe a mile from the bigger grassy place where I'd lived for a while before other folks come up there. I knew it was going to storm. It was dark an' there was a high wind howlin' farther up in the mountains. There was rain starting about the time I was half way along. But I had an old bear-cave I'd used other times so I figured to head for that an' was turning toward it down on the south side of the camping-meadow, walking through the trees. There was black rock down there stickin' up out of the ground. In daylight that didn't mean much, but as the storm got worse there got to be less an' less daylight.

"I was maybe three, four hundred feet along, walking west among the trees, when all at once there come this lightning. The sound was like a hundred men tearing bed-sheets. That's about all I remember except for a light so white you couldn't face it — everywhere. The trees looked like unlit candles. Terrible white. . . . That's all I remember."

Doc Mailer did not say a word. He did not move either for a long time. Eventually, without looking at the Templetons he went back by the stove and retrieved his coffee cup. After a while he faced the boy again and put aside the emptied cup.

"I'm going to cover your eyes with a bandage. You understand?"

Jim nodded his head.

"An' put some medicine on the bandage. I don't want you to take the bandage off, or raise it to let any light in."

Jim nodded again. He was sitting stiffly in the chair as Frank Mailer put his satchel on the table as he asked Nan if she had some hot water. She did have. "You can wash his face, with soap, especially up around his eyes."

Nan moved to obey and Jim raised his head slightly as she worked on him. Bart remained standing as Frank Mailer removed several items from his medicine bag. One of them was a pale green, square tin that had small flowers printed over the pale green. Bart recognized the tin. In fact he had several just like it down at the barn. He used the salve to help heal cuts on his horses.

He watched Doc Mailer unroll a length of heavy black cloth and use his finger to grease part of the cloth. Then Mailer straightened as Nan finished wiping Jim's face dry, and moved forward. "There's nothing to this," he told the boy. "It won't sting. It won't hurt at all. It's just to keep light out of your eyes for a few days."

Frank Mailer was an expert at bandaging; but then he'd been bandaging people most of his life. When he was finished and stepped back after testing the tightness of the cloth, he said, "How does it feel?"

Jim answered quietly. "Like something is wrapped around my head."

"Tight?"

"No. Well, not tight enough to hurt. I can smell the medicine. Will it cure me?"

Frank Mailer's expression changed for the first time since he'd entered the kitchen. He made a faint smile. "I don't know. I hope so. We won't know for a few days. Maybe by Sunday we can take it off and see if it's helped. Can you feel your way around until then?"

"Yes."

"And you won't lift the bandage or take it off?"

"No."

"Because it's very important, Jim, that you don't."

Mailer raised his eyes to Bart, made a little gesture with his hands, and was putting things back into his satchel before buckling it closed when Nan said she would make dinner. It was past noon, in fact, so it was reasonable to think everyone would be hungry.

Frank Mailer smiled at her on his way out of the kitchen. Bart followed him. They walked down to the barn where Dr. Mailer tied his satchel to the saddle he'd left astraddle of the saddle-pole. Bart was curious about that salve and pointed to an identical can on a shelf.

Frank Mailer gazed over there, then finished with the satchel, and faced around. "It's good stuff for cuts and scratches on horses, cattle, or men, but it can't make one damned bit of difference with that boy's eyes." At the solemn stare he was getting, Dr. Mailer added a little more to what he had already said. "It smells like medicine. Maybe Jim's never been to a redskin medicine man, and maybe he has, but anyway, they use herbs that their people associate with cures — medicine. Our people are damned little different. Knowing you have medicine on an injury convinces you that a cure is in process. Bart, healing folks is maybe as much as fifty percent in their minds. I know that from years of experience."

Bart's grave look did not change. "We're talkin' about a blind boy, Frank."

Dr. Mailer regarded Templeton for a moment, then said, "I'd feel better if we'd been able to keep the sun out of his face immediately after you folks found him in that dark cave. Still, it's too late to worry about that, so we'll take up where that should have begun and hope for the best."

"How much hope is there?" Bart asked, and the burly older man leaned across a saddle-seat on the pole as he replied. "Just as much as folks want to indulge in. But the rest of it's out of my hands as well as yours. Eyes are a hell of a lot different from broken bones or a case of the chicken pox. I don't suppose men would take any better care of them if they knew how damned delicate they are, an' that's why so many relatively young people wear eyeglasses. The best I can tell you is that there may be some hope. You absolutely cannot say much more in a case like this. I'll drive out in my buggy next Sunday and remove the bandage. Meanwhile, make him keep that bandage on. And there's one other thing you can do. Take him around the place with you. Stay with him. Talk about everything under the sun but mostly, make him feel like this is home and you want him to stay here for as long as he lives — or for as long as he wants to anyway. Bart? Keep his spirits up."

Dr. Mailer leaned a while longer across the saddle seat, gazing into the shadows across the barn runway. He wagged his head and straightened up. "I forgot to tell you. We buried those two Indian thieves day before yesterday. His kinsmen?"

"His brothers."

"Well, I wouldn't mention them if I were you, unless you can't keep from mentioning it. Y'know, it's a hell of a trip out here. Two days, and one night sleeping on the ground."

Bart understood. "I could bring him to Holtville."

Dr. Mailer shook his head. "Naw. But next time I'll use my buggy. It's not as hard on a man's behind. Anyway, I haven't looked in on John Holbrook in months. I ought to do that. I'll stop by his place on my way over here next Sunday."

Nan called from the veranda. Dinner was ready. They crossed the yard in silence. There was nothing more Frank Mailer could tell Bart about Jim's sight. He had not raised much hope, and that was bothering Bart as they climbed the steps to the veranda and entered the house.

Nan told them during the meal that her father had invited them over for Sunday dinner. Doc Mailer raised his eyes. He told her what he had told her husband down at the barn, and she seemed pleased. She said she and her family would probably be over at her father's place on Sunday, and that would shave a few miles off Doctor Mailer's drive.

When the meal was finished, the doctor lay a hand lightly on Jim's shoulder. "If the bandage slips or gets loose, ask Nan to snug it up again." He gave the thin shoulder a light slap and left the house with his host.

While they were rigging out Doc Mailer's big seal-brown mare, which was overweight but as gentle as a lamb, Mailer said, "I see Nan's about to worry herself sick over that boy. She'll most likely do a lot of crying into her pillow before this is settled. I don't have any medicine for that sort of thing; it'll be up to you."

Bart nodded in silence because he had already reached the same conclusion. As they were leading his horse out into the sunlight, though, he said, "She's got a hell of a mothering instinct, Frank."

Mailer heaved and grunted up into the saddle. He was a heavy man so it was fortunate the animal he was straddling weighed over a thousand pounds. He smiled about Bart's statement. "Then maybe someday you'll fill up the yard with youngsters." He thanked Bart for his hospitality, hauled his stud-necked big mare around, and rode west with the sun on his back. It was a long ride back. It was just as long coming out, but he'd had company then.

He toyed with the idea of stopping by the Holbrook yard but did not do it since he would be returning next Sunday.

Bart went down into the barn, kicked an empty horseshoe keg around, and sat on it, thinking. He was still perched like that when his wife came searching for him. She studied his face before saying, "He must not have been very encouraging."

Bart looked up at her. He checked himself from saying there was nothing to be encouraged about. Instead, he said, "About half of what he told me I don't understand. He said to keep Jim with me, take him around with me, keep his mind off things."

She leaned beside him. "Probably because he thinks it will help later when the bandage is taken off, if he's felt good for a few days."

Bart accepted that as a possibility and stood up. "They buried his brothers in the Holtville cemetery."

She mentioned Jim's wish that they could have been buried on the ranch. She also said, "I told him it might be possible. Now I'll have to tell him they have already been buried — sixty miles from here."

"Well, don't tell him before Sunday, unless he asks. I expect we'd better do as Frank said, make him feel thoroughly at home, make him as happy as we can."

She said, "Sunday. When my father rode over to invite us to supper, I liked the idea. All of us being together, good food, a pleasant time."

"And now?"

She looked at him with pain-shadowed eyes. "And now we'll ride over, the bandage will come off . . ."

She fell into his arms, burrowing her face against his chest to muffle the sobs. He held her gently, gazing out across the drying yard in the direction Doc Mailer had ridden. He was no longer in sight. Except for some loose horses grazing quite a ways out, there was nothing moving at all.

He had never been an individual who cursed fate, but right now he was tempted.

He recognized his remount stallion out there. She had not told him of his visit to the yard with his mares and foals. As the sobs subsided and she pushed away to raise a balled up handkerchief to her face, he thought of the time he had been riding the big wild horse from the mesa when his remount stud had started a battle. The only ultimate casualty of that horse fight had been Bart, for although Big Ben had been knocked senseless, he had recovered much faster than Bart had. Ben had got a dent in his forehead as a result of that fight, but Bart had been forced to do everything with one arm until his broken arm had healed.

CHAPTER 21
LIVING WITH IT

Bart had several chores to take care of involving his team and wagon. He loaded poles and tools, handed Jim up beside him on the seat, and left the yard heading northwesterly.

It was another magnificent day. He almost commented about this, then bit his tongue.

It was difficult making conversation, but he persevered. They talked about horses, something Bart knew about and something the Indian boy was interested in. Bart told him horse stories until they reached the first silted-up spring where his horses watered. As he climbed down to lift out the tools he needed, he said, "When I was about your age, an old man gave me a chew of molasses-cured cut plug." He said no more until he was over at the spring ready to dig out silt. There, leaning on the shovel and admiring the day, the wild, free flow of open country, he finally returned to his narrative. "I'd watched the old man tear off a corner, so I did the same. Thing is, the old man had been chewing all his life. He knew exactly how to tear off a small piece. Me, well, when it came loose I had a piece of chewing tobacco about as big as a couple of fingers are wide. The old man was watching, nodding approval. Well, that stuff stung the inside of my mouth, so the saliva built up and directly I had such a mouthful of tobacco juice my cheeks was puffed out like a chipmunk."

Jim said, "Why didn't you spit it out?"

Bart leaned on the shovel. "That was the problem. You see that old man said he didn't buy good Kentucky twist just to spit it on the ground. So I dassn't spit."

"What did you do?"

"Swallowed the juice. It went part way down. I felt like a mule had kicked me in the middle of the chest. I couldn't breathe. I was sitting down or I'd have dropped like a pole-axed steer. Then I got sick. The sicker I got, the louder the old man laughed. I got so sick and felt so miserable I thought I'd die and wished I would."

Jim was leaning forward on the wagon seat in the direction of Bart's voice. "What happened?"

"Not much. I couldn't even keep water down for the rest of that day, but the next day I was all right. But I'll tell you one thing, from that day to this I never, ever, took another chew of tobacco."

"What about the old man?"

"Oh, he told everyone he came across about it and was still laughin' a year later when I left that country."

Jim was quiet for a long time. Bart had cleaned the spring and was pitching the tools back behind the seat onto the wagon bed before he spoke. "Did you ever smoke?"

Bart shook his head, remembered Jim could not see that, and said, "Nope. I just never cared for the smell of smoking tobacco. Did you ever try it?"

Jim had. "Yes, my father kept shag in a pouch he wore on his belt. He'd hang the pouch on a pole when he went to bed. I liked the smell of his smokin' tobacco, so I stole some one time while he was sleeping, and the next day rolled a cigarette. I didn't throw up, but I got so dizzy I kept falling down. My mother thought I'd got hold of some whiskey. She scolded me real bad and sent me to bed without supper."

Bart laughed, stepped onto the wheel hub, and came up beside the youth. Jim did not laugh but he was smiling as they drove more southward in the direction of a stand of sugar pines. Bart racked his brain for other interludes in his youth, and finally got Jim to laugh as he told him about the Sunday when everyone had just finished a big dinner and the older men saddled a four-hundred-pound steer in a corral and shoved him down into the saddle.

He had been afraid to allow himself to be bucked off for fear the steer would trample him, so he had used both hands to hang on with while his head snapped like an apple on a string as the steer bawled and bucked every way but straight ahead.

Jim laughed.

"Then," stated Bart, "the confounded thing decided that since he couldn't shake me off, he'd brush me off. He ran completely around that corral leaning as hard as he could against the stringers. I thought he'd busted my leg about ten times before he quit and someone jumped down, grabbed his head, and tipped it up until I could unload. I couldn't stand up."

"Was the leg broke?"

"No, but every time one of the men would touch it I'd scream bloody murder. Eventually my ma came down there because of the yelling, and when she was finished with my pa and the others, they slunk down into the barn like whipped dogs. You know, Jim, I limped on that leg for two weeks. I was so pitiful my ma took me into town and made me fried chicken. I sure hated to give up that limp."

The boy laughed again, then raised a hand

to his face. "Were you ever unable to see?" he asked.

Bart looked sideways quickly before answering. "No, I never was. There was another time: I had a cousin who was real fat. He was bigger and older'n I was. He used to whip me about two, three times a week. Right up to the time we was in a hayloft at his folks' farm, up in the mow, and I slipped his suspenders over the tines of the Jackson fork and gave him a boot in the rear. You could have heard him holler all the way to Kansas as he sailed out the barn maw and hung out there, flappin' like a bird."

Jim smiled and looked around. "Did you get him down?"

"Nope. That time it was my ma and pa, and after he was on the ground and told them I'd hooked his suspenders over the fork, they went after me like the Devil after a crippled saint."

Jim laughed. "What happened the next time you met him?"

Bart sighed. "He whipped me."

They hauled up at the first of the trees, Bart climbed down for the tools again, and this time Jim also climbed down. He felt along the sideboards to the tailgate and asked if he could help. Bart handed him a shovel, helped him through the mud, and showed him where to dig. They talked as they shoveled silt. When Bart said the water was flowing again, they returned to the rig, tossed in their tools, and climbed back to the seat. Jim asked if there were any more springs that needed cleaning, and Bart, aiming the team for home, said they had cleaned the only two his horses used. He did not mention the mud on his trousers and his shirt where Jim had unknowingly flung mud.

As they were entering the yard, Jim turned his bandaged eyes and said, "I helped."

Bart looked around, put a powerful arm around the boy's shoulders and agreed. "You sure did, Jim. Remember that story Mr. Holbrook told you about the feller he knew who was blind?"

"Yes. If you go out tomorrow, could I come along?"

Bart lied like a Dutch uncle. "I was just goin' to ask if you'd ride with me tomorrow. I'd sort of like to know where the mares and colts are."

"Ride?" the boy said with a fading voice.

"Sure. You know how to ride and rein a horse. I know you do because we rode together before." He ended it lamely, then hurried ahead so Jim would not remember where they had ridden together before. "The horse can do all the seeing you got to do. . . .

I'd like to pass by some salt logs, too. If they're empty, I expect day after tomorrow we can hitch up the wagon and haul salt out there." He was watching for the shadow that did not appear. He had successfully prevented Jim from thinking about their last horseback ride together. He said, "If a man puts out salt, he don't usually have too much trouble finding his livestock. Cattle and horses love salt. They never get enough from natural sources."

Nan was waiting for them. She stared at her mud-splattered husband. He raised a finger to his lips and climbed down to take care of the horses. Nan took Jim back to the house with her. Bart watched them. They were chattering like magpies as they reached the veranda.

He went out back to the trough before going to the house, sluiced off most of the mud, then fed the corralled horses and leaned there in warm, fading daylight listening to them eat.

Nan came around the side of the barn and also looked in at the horses. "What happened?"

"Well, he wanted to help shovel the mud out. We were talking most of the time, and I guess he forgot where the sound of my voice was coming from. He pitched mud on me twice before I could get un-tracked and get out of the way."

She looked him up and down, then leaned on the corral stringers laughing. He eyed her ruefully. "I was supposed to get Jim to laughing, not you."

She raised up and wiped her eyes. "Why not me? I need it too." She touched his cheek. "That's the most life I've ever seen in him, Bart. He says you're going to take him out on horseback tomorrow."

"Yeah. Ride around in a big five-mile circle and pretend like I'm lookin' for the horses."

She nodded and raised an arm. "Then don't go east because that's where Ben had his harem yesterday."

He nodded. He had seen Big Ben out there when she had been crying in his arms.

She turned back to watch the corralled horses. "It breaks my heart."

He nodded. "Yeah, I understand. But you know, there really are things he can do when he's not thinkin' about being blind."

She faced him nodding, trying to smile through a blur of tears. He took her by the hand and started toward the house. To help her regain control he said, "Cleaning springs makes a man hungry. Tonight I'll bet he eats twice as much as he usually does."

She dabbed at her eyes and smiled. "In that case we're going to have to drive over to Holtville for supplies long before autumn."

He left her in the parlor while he went to change clothes. He could hear the two of them talking out in the kitchen. For a moment after he had redressed he stood by the second of only two windows in his house looking out, watching the first faint sootiness of dusk settle, seeing beyond it a faint light where an occasional star shone. He knew about some Indians pulling their "medicine" from particular stars. He looked for the brightest one up there and breathed a combination plea and prayer, then went along to the kitchen where Nan's cooking had filled most of the house with aromas that made him especially conscious of being hungry.

Jim's light mood remained until bedtime. When the fires had been damped down, the lamps blown out, the house was quiet and beyond, out across the yard, a thickening moon shed soft, eerie light, Nan turned to her husband in bed and smiled. "You never told me those stories; the one about your fat cousin and the one about the old man and the chewing tobacco."

He chuckled. "You're lucky. Maybe after we've been married a long time you'll flinch when I start reminiscing. I've noticed folks keep telling the same stories over and over."

She watched moonlight dapple the far wall. "You have never told me where you grew up, or anything about your family."

"Missouri," he said, "until I was a couple of years older'n Jim. Then I hired on with that old man who gave me the lesson about chewing tobacco. He was a traveling cattle dealer. I did the herding for him. When I got as far as Council Bluffs, I quit the old man and hired on with a freight company hauling goods out here. I left the freight outfit and worked the ranges from Montana on south. The rest of it you know. I quit riding for other people, took up on this land, and here I am. Nothing very colorful, and it don't take long to tell it."

"What about your family?" she asked, and he turned his head on the pillow. "How come you're not sleepy? I am. I dug mud today. That tires a man."

She smothered laughter. He regarded her for a moment, knew she was remembering how woebegone he had looked when they returned to the yard, mud clinging to him, and turned up onto his side as he said, "Good night."

She replied and also got settled, but five minutes later she suddenly said, "I don't want to go over to the ranch Sunday."

He opened his eyes, squinted at moonshine on the wall, collected his wits, and said, "Why not?"

"I just don't."

He lay a moment gazing at the moonlight. "You don't want to go because you don't want to be there when Frank Mailer takes the bandage off."

She did not deny it. She sounded almost defiant when she said, "Do you?"

"Well, not exactly, but not goin' or not seeing the bandage come off won't change anything. And if we don't show up Sunday, sure as hell he'll ride over here, so what would we gain by stayin' home? Maybe a couple more hours of not knowing."

She remained silent. He groped for her hand, their fingers entwined, and sleep came to them both.

In the morning Jim had groped his way to the wash house before anyone was stirring. He was out in the kitchen building a kindling wood fire in the stove when Nan came to the doorway to watch, and he looked toward the door as he said, "Am I doin' it right?"

She wanted to run to him and hold him against her. "Exactly right," she said.

"Then I'll go fetch a bucket of water," he said, as the stove began to crackle. She watched him go unerringly toward the rear door, open it, and disappear outside with a bucket in one hand. She went to the stove and got busy, carrying with her a heartache big enough for two people.

Bart fed the horses, watched Jim crank up a bucketful of water from the well, thought the bandage over his eyes should be tightened, and went back down into the barn.

It was Friday but Bart did not realize it until Nan told him after breakfast when Jim was in the parlor putting on his old sweater. He was standing by the stove drinking his second cup of coffee when she told him that. He considered the cup. He did not always know what day of the week it was. In fact, he rarely knew. He did not work according to the days of the week, he worked according to what had to be done.

She said, "I'm going to get gray hair."

He looked at her. She was lithe, leggy, full bodied and very handsome. "I wouldn't care if you got bald."

She swept a gaze in his direction, smiling a little. "You are so — fatalistic."

He finished the coffee, put the cup in the tub of heating wash water on the stove, and went after his hat. If he had told her his insides were just as knotted as hers were, she wouldn't have believed him. He pecked her on the cheek and went through the parlor, talking to Jim.

As the door closed she went to the single parlor window and watched them striding side by side in the direction of the barn. They

287

were talking; her husband laughed a couple of times, and Jim looked up at the sound of his voice and smiled. She could see him do that.

She returned to the kitchen and got busy. It was probably going to be another idyllic early summertime day. She should take advantage of this by hauling the blankets and bedding out behind the house where an old lariat had been stretched, and beat them. She was not fond of housework, but to-day, and probably tomorrow as well, it would be a godsend because it would keep her busy, and after supper tonight she would be too tired to lie awake as she had done last night.

She was finishing in the kitchen when she heard a horse nicker and returned to the parlor window. Her husband and Jim were leaving the yard side by side, her husband watching the boy's horse and occasionally gesturing as he spoke, neglecting to remember that Jim could not see him do that.

The sun arrived, flooding Nan's world with brilliance and a promise of heat later that day. The sky was pale turquoise without a blemish from one horizon to the other.

She took a long last look at her men angling at a steady walk toward the northwesterly range and turned fiercely away, going in search of the wire rug-beater. What she could not take out on fate she could certainly take out on blankets and cotton mattresses with that rug-beater.

CHAPTER 22
THE PRICE OF TERROR

She dreaded every step of the horses pulling the wagon in the direction of her father's yard on Sunday. She did not notice what a magnificent morning it was. Her silence infected both Bart and Jim. For a half hour as he drove along, hunched forward on the spring-seat, Bart made no attempt to change things, but eventually he did, when a big bobcat sprang out of some underbrush and went streaking southward with great, graceful bounds. He did not mention the bobcat, but he straightened back on the seat and looked at the boy sitting between them.

Jim was facing forward, his face expressionless, his mouth held closed without pressure, his hands in his lap like dead birds. Bart tapped Jim's leg as he said, "Darned few guarantees in this life, Jim. Darned few answers about why things happen, as well. But here we are and here we'll stay until our rope runs out. Some folks are luckier'n others an' no one knows why that is, but every one of us has got somethin' special, an' that's what we got to find out about, then make it work for us."

Nan gave him a disapproving glance, almost an angry one. He settled back and watched the undulating rumps of the team. Maybe her disapproval was warranted. Maybe just moping along in silence was best, because there really were no words, that he knew anyway, to make a bridge between what the boy had known since birth, and what he had lost up on Wild Horse Mesa.

But it was hard not to want to at least try to prepare Jim for what probably was up ahead in John Holbrook's yard.

There were meadow larks in the grass. Their song was musically loud. The air was fragrant from wild flowers, some so tiny it was hard to see them, like the lavender alfilaria petals. They had rooftops and tall old trees in sight when Jim suddenly said, "The happiest days I remember have been since I came down off the mesa."

Bart did not dare look at his wife, which was just as well because she had turned her face away and was looking southward.

John Holbrook's lanky rangeboss, Charley Lord, loped out to meet them. As he swung in beside the wagon, he leaned from the saddle as he said, "Hey Jim, you ever eaten turkey with stuffing? It's waitin' up yonder."

The boy turned in the direction of Lord's voice, and smiled, but he said nothing.

As they entered the yard, the *cocinero* watched from the porch of the main house. Two riders came to the barn to help Bart with the outfit while Nan climbed down and held up a hand to Jim, who hesitated before allowing her to steer him down to the hub. After that he released her hand and turned as a rough voice said, "Boy, you been puttin' on weight. Last time I saw you there wasn't enough of you to cast a shadow."

Jim knew the voice. "How is your face?" he asked, and Cuff answered in the same warm, rough tone of voice: "Pretty as a picture. I'm thinkin' about goin' back to pose for them Montgomery Ward catalogs."

The rider named Fred spoke up. "He's lyin', Jim. He don't look one bit better'n he ever did."

John Holbrook arrived and with him Dr. Mailer. Nan had to force herself to look at Mailer. Her father took Jim's arm and started in the direction of the main house. Frank Mailer smiled at Nan as she moved past him to follow. When the horses had been taken off the pole into the barn to be cared for, the doctor looked at Bart across the old wagon and said, "How has he been?"

Bart shrugged. "Happy, I guess. Leastways when we ride out together he talks and laughs. On the drive over he said the happiest times he can remember have been since we brought him home with us."

Dr. Mailer nodded about that and turned away, walking toward the main house.

Charley Lord and Cuff came out of the barn and stopped at the hitchrack. Bart faced them uncertainly. "It's pretty damned hard," he told them, and they nodded. Charley reset his hat before speaking. "Does he set around?"

"No, he goes out with me in the wagon an' on horseback."

"I expect then that maybe he's accepting it. To tell you the truth, Bart, he don't really act In'ian most of the time."

Cuff had a comment to make about that. "He hasn't been around 'em lately."

Charley did not quite accept that as the explanation. "Sixteen years around them," he said. "I don't think that's it, Cuff. I think he's just not a hell of a lot like some In'ians I've run across."

"Well, there's no reason why they got to all be alike," replied the man with the faintly scarred face.

Bart looked at Charley. "Have you talked to Frank?"

Lord hadn't. "He just got here maybe an hour back, an' since then he's been up at the main house. But sure as hell he's talked to John."

Charley straightened up, waiting for whatever else Bart had to say. Cuff asked a question. "How's your wife takin' it?"

Bart looked at the shorter, older man. "About like you'd expect a woman to take it. Good days and bad days."

Charley jutted his chin. "Why don't you go over and talk to Frank?"

"Because," Bart answered honestly, "I'm afraid to."

They left him to head for the bunkhouse to clean up before dinner. Dr. Mailer came down from the main house porch, the only man moving across the yard. When Bart leaned on the hitchrack watching Mailer approach, his legs felt weak. What was worrying at him was less the knowledge of what Frank might say than it was the damned uncertainty; it had been gnawing at him for a long time now. He'd been able to control it right up until he'd stopped the wagon in front of the Holbrook barn; then his control diminished.

Mailer did not smile as he came up and said, "John's sweating. He's got a big turkey dinner over there."

"We'll all eat," Bart told him.

"Yeah, but there's a hell of a cloud of tension, Bart. John asked me whether I should examine the lad before dinner or after."

Bart looked at the ground for a moment before answering. "Either way there's likely to be a hell of a lot of turkey left over."

Mailer agreed with that. "If it'd been up to me, I wouldn't have done it like this. I'd just have driven to your place with only you and Nan, the boy and me. But John's different."

Bart made a wooden smile. "He is for a fact. Well, which is it going to be — before or after?"

"That's why I came down here. It's not just the boy that stands to lose, it's you and your wife. Which way would you prefer?"

Bart straightened up gazing in the direction of the main house. "To tell you the truth, Frank, I don't think Nan can stand much more of this, an' I know for a fact I can't."

Mailer nodded. "Now, then?"

"Yes. And get it over with."

"Come on back to the house with me. I've got my satchel in one of the bedrooms."

Dr. Mailer was already turning when Bart stopped him with a question. "Any hope at all?"

Mailer turned back. "We discussed that business of hoping before, remember? I can't

295

add anything to what we said back then. But, well, let's go get this damned thing over with."

They approached the main house side by side, went up the steps of the porch, and entered the house. Nan was in the kitchen with the ranch cook. Jim and John Holbrook were over by the hearth quietly talking. They both looked up as Mailer and Templeton entered. Nan did not glance out from the kitchen. She was shiny-faced because the kitchen was too hot. Bart thought she was almost frantically busy.

Dr. Mailer crossed to the fireplace, nodded to John Holbrook, and lay a hand upon the boy's shoulder as he said, "Jim, let's go in a back room and take the bandage off."

The adults stopped moving, but Jim raised his head in the direction of Mailer's voice, and allowed himself to be steered away by the doctor's hand on his shoulder. As they were entering a long, shadowy hallway Dr. Mailer looked back. "Bart?" he said. Templeton exchanged a look with his father-in-law, then dutifully followed Doctor Mailer and Jim.

The bedroom Dr. Mailer had left his bag in had clearly not been used for a number of years, and even though someone had opened a small window in the rear wall, a lingering smell of mustiness remained.

Mailer put his back to the little window and looked gravely at the boy for a moment, then he turned him so that his back was also to the window and guided him to a chair. He ignored Bart's presence entirely as he opened his leather bag. When he spoke, it was to the boy.

"Have you taken the bandage off?"

Jim's back was to both the older men when he replied. "No."

"Maybe just to tip it up a little?"

This time the answer was slower coming. "I had to scratch a couple of times."

Dr. Mailer continued to grope in his satchel without looking up from what he was doing. "And maybe there was a little light came in?"

Jim did not hesitate this time, "No."

Finally, Doctor Mailer raised his head in the boy's direction, and cast a fleeting glance toward Bart. He did not speak again until he was behind the chair ready to cut the bandage off. "Now then," he said, "it's been dark under there for quite a spell, so when we remove the bandage it's going to seem different. What I want you to tell me is how much different. What kind of a difference there is."

Jim answered without moving. "Yes."

Bart looked around for something to sit on. There was only the one chair so he went to the foot of the bed and sat down over there.

Mailer worked carefully at removing the bandage. His hands were as steady as stones. Bart marvelled that he could be so business-like. It dawned on him now how Frank had managed to be so successful last year in removing that bird arrowpoint from John Holbrook's spine. If he was wound tight inside he managed to control it very well.

Jim was facing the wall when the bandage was finally taken off. He had his eyes closed, perhaps from dread, perhaps because he was accustomed to having them closed beneath the black bandage.

Frank Mailer put the bandage beside his satchel on a small table, stepped around between Jim and the wall and looked surprised. "Why do you keep your eyes closed?" he asked.

"Because — I think they hurt."

Mailer looked at Bart with an expression Bart had not expected. It was a look of guarded triumph. He leaned and said, "Jim, look at me."

For five seconds there was not a sound in the room, then Jim quietly said, "I can see you. Not real clear, but I know what you're doing."

"What am I doing?"

"Smiling."

Frank straightened up very slowly looking

over the chair back to the man sitting at the foot of the old bed. "Go get your wife," he said. "I'll be down at the barn."

He left the room, walked across the parlor to the door without looking at anyone, closed the door after himself and went briskly across the sunbright yard to the barn where his buggy had been pulled into the shade.

He rummaged beneath the buggy seat, brought forth a small pony of brandy, took two swallows that burned all the way down, capped the bottle, and put it back inside the folds of his buggy robe beneath the seat. Then he walked out back as far as an old stone water trough and sat down with hot sunlight on his shoulders and head, and closed his eyes with his lips barely moving. He only looked up when he heard bootsteps approaching down the barn runway. When Bart appeared, Frank nodded at him.

The horsebreaker went over to the trough and sat down without saying a word for a moment or two, and when he finally spoke he looked squarely at the older man.

"You knew, didn't you?"

Mailer blew out a fiery breath and wagged his head. "No. There wasn't any way to know, but I'll explain something to you I could have told you a couple of weeks ago, except that I was afraid to.

"Over at your place he told us he was walking in some trees at the south end of the glade. It was raining, he said, and there were rocks, and it was dark or getting dark. And he said he was a fair distance from where that lighting struck; he was walking west to find his cave."

Bart nodded.

"Well, I made a guess. He wasn't facing the lightning when it flashed; he was looking among the trees. And he didn't get struck by the lightning; he was probably in a hurry to get out of the rain and into the cave. He took a hell of a fall over some rocks. That's how he hurt his side. I had to look it up to find out just how close someone had to be to lightning for it to lift him and fling him through the air. There wasn't anything definite in the books I read, but the idea seemed to be that a person had to be real close — and he wasn't, was he? So — it had to be that he was hurrying in the dark and fell over one of those big rocks, bounced off a tree and bruised his side."

Bart sat perfectly still, saying nothing.

Frank Mailer turned toward him. "Remember what he said about the trees looking like white candles after the bolt hit?"

"Yes."

"If the lightning had blinded him, it would have done it then and there, immediately. He wouldn't have been able to see what the trees looked like — unless he was looking at them, and if he did that, why then, he wasn't facing the lightning when it struck."

Bart sat back looking at the older man. "Frank, he was blind. When we found him up there, we had to lead him around. We still had to right up until today."

Mailer did not dispute this. He arose because the sun was hot out where there was no shade, and took Bart with him back to the buggy. There, he rummaged for the pony of brandy, offered it to Bart, who took a swallow, then Mailer took another two swallows, and this time he panted like a dog as he stoppered the little bottle and shoved it back under the buggy seat.

He faced around and leaned on the buggy. It was ten degrees cooler in the barn than it had been out back by the stone trough. "Nothing worse for a man on a hot day than brandy," he said, and saw the expressionless look on Templeton's face. He hung fire for a moment, frowning to himself, before he finally started speaking again.

"I've been at my trade a long time, Bart. Back east I did a lot of studying. I had quite a reputation back there. But that's neither here nor there.

"I've got to explain this so's it makes sense, so bear with me. All right?"

Bart woodenly nodded.

Dr. Mailer frowned in the direction of the yard for a moment, clearly ordering his thoughts so that when he expressed them they would make sense. Still looking toward the yard, he finally said, "I expect this is going to sound like something straight out of Alice in Wonderland, but it isn't. I've read of this happening, and I've seen it happen twice." Frank finally brought his gaze back to Templeton and held it there. "The boy's had a series of jolts lately. First up there with Abel, Foster, and Alex. He saw Abel darn near die. Before that he saw Alex point a gun at him. Then the two of you ran yourselves ragged down to that emigrant's camp. From there you came here and got horses, guns, and some men. He went with you on a hell of a hard ride after some horse thieves. He was down there with you when the killing started." Frank paused, still looking straight at Bart Templeton. "Then you came back here. John and Charley told me all this, blow by blow. The next morning he went down to the barn, looked at those dead horse thieves, and got another shock, only this one was probably the worst shock he'd ever had in his life. Two of those dead thieves were his brothers." Frank paused again, looked out into the sunshine and back before finishing what he had to say.

"I'd guess he didn't sleep at all that night. Shock can do strange things to people. I've seen them drop everything and go running wildly, screaming at the top of their voices. I've also seen them get a glassy look and drop to the ground unconscious. In this case, the effect was building up all night. In the morning he took a horse and went riding toward the only place he knew of where there was peace — and got up there right when a hell of a storm hit. The lightning struck. I think that completed the shock, the deep-down, paralyzing shock. He was hurt, stunned, and absolutely alone. His system reacted in this way: after the lightning struck, it was completely overwhelmed. Instead of sending him wildly screaming through the night, it turned inward. Sure, the lighting temporarily blinded him, but in the same way it would someone who didn't have all those internal things building up to an internal explosion.

"He was on his hands and knees still blinded by the flash, but when you or I would have recovered from the brilliance, he didn't. He was crawling, probably whimpering, and scared to death. His system reacted by keeping him blind. . . . Sounds pretty crazy, doesn't it?"

Bart said nothing, but he turned to find something to lean on.

Frank Mailer kept on. "In wars men get so terrified and overwhelmed, they drop to the ground unconscious. But twice in my lifetime I've seen an uncontrollable inner shock to the nervous system manifest in physical ways. Once, it was heaving — dry wretching until blood came. Another time it was tremors that lasted for several days, so the man almost convulsed to death. This time, it manifested in an outlet of inner screaming by perpetuating what already aided the final shock. It kept him blind long after his eyes would have recovered from the oblique brilliance of lightning."

As Dr. Mailer finished speaking, both he and Bart heard loud voices coming from the direction of the main house. Loud, excited, almost hysterically happy voices.

Bart leaned on a saddle pole, gazing at the physician. He finally smiled. "Tell you something, Frank. If I was a praying man, I'd get down on my knees."

Mailer's response was dry. "You could try it anyway. It never hurt anyone, and occasionally it helps. That's what I was doing out back on the trough when you came along."

"Will it last? Will his vision stay clear?"

"I'd say it would, Bart. In fact from what I know about things like this, it doesn't happen twice to the same person, without the same set of circumstances cropping up, and hell, I'd say that's such a remote possibility that it'll never happen."

"I was wondering about damage to the eyes, Frank. Something that may not show up for a few years."

Dr. Mailer flapped his arms and looked exasperated. "There is no way I can tell you any more than I already have. I can't give you any guarantees, Bart. Maybe, by the time he's my age he might need glasses, and maybe that won't have anything to do with his experience. Bart, I just don't know." Mailer eyed the robe beneath the buggy seat but made no move toward it. "I'm not even certain my diagnosis about the return of his eyesight is correct. I just know that the boy can see, and I for one will accept that as a blessing, whatever in hell caused it."

Someone was striding loudly from the direction of the main house. It was John Holbrook looking slightly flushed. He stopped at the solemn expressions of the two men down by the saddle pole, then approached. "Frank, you made another miracle," he said, looking from one of them to the other. "Is something wrong?"

Bart pointed to a small keg. "Sit down, John. What Frank has been tellin' me made my legs weak."

Holbrook did not sit; he went over and leaned on the buggy, though, waiting for Doc Mailer to explain.

Frank expelled a rattling long breath. He did not want to go through it again but John Holbrook, who had more than befriended him last year, was clearly waiting. He started speaking, and during this second explanation Bart wandered out back, then shuffled thoughtfully in the direction of the house. He wanted to be with his wife.

CHAPTER 23
A MATTER OF PLANNING

It was more than a feast. It was a genuine thanksgiving, and it lasted until sundown when Nan and her husband had to leave. There were chores waiting at home. Everyone came to the barn to see them off and Cuff was nudging Charley Lord as the Templetons climbed to the wagon seat. Charley went briskly to the bunkhouse and came back briskly carrying a new manila lass rope, properly coiled and with the Turk's-head knot already braided in the dally end, and the braided hondo at the other end. He leaned and placed the rope on Jim's lap. "From the riders," he said and got red in the face as the boy picked up his lariat and held it tightly as he looked at the rangeman. His chin quivered and Cuff said, "It ain't much. We just thought we'd keep it around until maybe someday you could use it. Boy, I never been happier about somethin' turning out right than I am right now."

The rangeman smiled, and one of them said, "But if you really want to learn to use that thing, Jim, you got to come back over here an' we'll teach you. Horse breakers don't keep their hands in like us fellers do who work cattle an' got to work with lass ropes every few days. So you come back, hear?"

John Holbrook and Frank Mailer stood in unsmiling silence. Nan looked at them through blurry vision. When Jim said, "Thank you," in an unusually high tone of voice, Nan smiled at her father and Dr. Mailer. "I can't tell you how I feel. You are wonderful, both of you — all of you."

Bart eased the binder off and talked up the horses. He turned once to raise a hand to his hat brim, then sat forward for the drive home.

The men in the Holbrook yard were like crows on a fence for a long while, until the *cocinero* said, "John, there's enough grub left for us to gnaw on for several days."

Holbrook nodded absently, still watching the distant wagon.

The cook then added another sentence. "An' a real host would take everyone over to the house to help him get rid of them half empty bottles too."

Holbrook turned slowly to regard his cook, then nodded his head and led the way. They

308

were on the porch when John repeated what he had said earlier in the barn. "Frank, you made another miracle."

Mailer reddened. He stopped where they could all see and hear him and said, "Miracle my butt. If I'd never opened my mouth, if I'd never come out here this morning, the lad still would have had his eyesight back. I had nothing to do with it — except to take off that damned bandage — an' an idiot could have done that much."

The men regarded Doc Mailer owlishly. They knew he was annoyed without being able to understand why, and he stalked into the house without explaining. But his reason was as old as his profession. The most ruinous thing people could believe about a medical practitioner was that he could work miracles, because he couldn't and sooner or later folks would realize it, and the fall from the pedestal could destroy him. It had happened hundreds of times, but it was worse when some doctor allowed his ego to believe that fallacy. It was much better to angrily denounce any such notion, as Frank Mailer had done.

Daylight was fading, but its warmth remained and probably would continue to remain until after darkness arrived. Springtime had yielded to full summer, days were longer, hotter, and the only time it was cold was long after sundown.

Nan came to the barn with a lantern while Bart and Jim took the horses off the pole, draped the harness and turned the animals into a corral out back where other horses were waiting impatiently to be fed. Bart sent Jim to the house with his wife and fed the horses by himself. Then he removed his hat and took Frank Mailer's advice about giving solemn and prayerful thanks.

There were white stars. He looked up and recalled something an old Mexican had once told him in all sincerity. Stars were actually holes in the fabric that the floor of heaven was made of. Like moth holes. And above the moth-eaten old fabric was heaven with brilliant gold light everlasting, and that was what shone through the holes and people called stars.

He dropped his hat back on and leaned to listen to the horses eating. Because the days would be longer now, maybe he and Jim could start hauling logs for that lean-to room. He gazed northward. Or maybe they should go back to Wild Horse Mesa and trap some horses. They couldn't do that after autumn freezes arrived, but frost would not stop them from building the lean-to. Like just about everything in this life, if a man didn't understand that things had to be done by sequence, in an orderly way, his life would always be helter skelter.

He hiked to the house where Nan was boiling coffee and talking to Jim, who had his new lariat on the kitchen table in front of the place where he was sitting. When they both turned as he entered, he saw the shining happiness in their eyes. Even guttering coal-oil lamps could not hide it.

Nan filled a cup for him and put it at the place where he usually sat. He winked at Jim. "They was right when they told you cattlemen use lariats a lot oftener than horsemen do. But then, I was a rangeman for a long while before I settled down to the horse business, so maybe I can teach you how to use that thing."

Nan made a statement that had nothing to do with roping. She said, "He wants me to cut his hair. He wants to wear it like you do, like my father's riders wear theirs."

Bart had an abrupt and inexplicable twinge. He drank coffee until it passed and the thought which had come with it sobered him. There were white Indians, redskins who wore white men's clothing and had their hair cut to match the way whiteskins wore their hair. He had seen them ridiculed in towns. He gazed at Jim thinking that ahead, perhaps before too long, he was going to encounter that. Among rangemen Indian riders were teased but there was no ridicule, unless, of course, they missed a cast with their ropes, or got bucked off a horse, but the same hooting was used against other riders, white or Mex or whatever they were. If Jim spent his life on the range, he would encounter a minimum of that ridicule. But towns were different.

He drained the cup and put it aside, sat gazing at the rapidly growing boy, and allowed Jim's and Nan's unquenchable happiness to carry him along. But he also thought of something else and was still thinking of it when they blew down the lamp mantles and went to bed.

Nan knelt at bedside. He had never seen her do that before. When she climbed in beside him, she said, "I had to thank someone."

He did not comment. The difference was that he had not knelt, and it had been corral stringers not a bed he had leaned upon when he had done the identical thing.

"Bart?"

"Yes."

"I thought on the drive back that if I live to be very old, no matter what happens to make me happy, it probably can never make me as happy as I've been today."

He felt for her hand and held it beneath the blankets. "We put a lot of salt in those logs up on the mesa," he said.

She was totally silent for as long as it took her to make the adjustment to his comment, which had been about as alien to her comment and the feelings she had felt, as any words could be.

He took her silence for interest. "It's a shame to leave that salt up there for every varmint under the sun to eat."

She turned her head on the pillow, studied his profile by the weak starshine, and finally said, "You want to go back up there and trap some horses." It was not a question; it was a statement of fact.

"Well, Jim'd get a chance to use his rope, maybe, and we did go up there with the salt to scout for wild horses, didn't we?"

She had no objection; it was just that he was being practical at a time when she was being emotional. "Yes," she murmured. "I wonder about the wisdom of taking Jim up there so soon."

He faced her on the pillow. "I don't think it'll bother him. I'll keep him busy."

"When?" she asked.

"In a couple of days. After he and I've ridden the range to make certain Ben and his mares are all right."

She lay still, looking at a square of white light on the far wall. "We really should go over to Holtville, Bart. We're getting very low

313

on just about everything but meat."

It was his turn to be silent for a long moment. He'd had his mind on Wild Horse Mesa. But she was probably right. It would use up the best part of a week going to Holtville and back. He had never been enthusiastic about that trek, but he agreed with her as another thought came to him. "All right. We can leave real early day after tomorrow. And there's somethin' that needs to be done in town."

"Yes?"

"Get him some new boots an' some decent pants and shirts. Maybe a jacket or a coat to replace that old sweater."

She said, "Day after tomorrow. Good night."

"Good night."

"Bart?"

"Yes."

"Do you suppose he's ever been in a town as large as Holtville before?"

"Maybe not, but better now than when he's much older. I never cared much for towns either, but they got their uses."

"Good night."

"Good night, Nan."

"Bart?"

"Yes."

"I love you."

He squeezed her hand and hitched over onto his side.

A band of foraging coyotes passed through not too far from the yard, pausing to sit back and sound at the moon, then hurried along, their sharp fox faces and never still tawny eyes looking southward in the direction of the yard with its mingled scents. The one scent they wanted to catch was lacking. Nan did not keep chickens.

The last sounds they made were from maybe two miles out, still northward but also eastward, as they ran in a ragged split hoping to start up nocturnal mice, or if they were very lucky, a ground-owl, which they rarely found because ground-owls were usually airborne at this time of night, also foraging.

Thirty miles northward the aura of a pale moon amid clusters of stars outlined Wild Horse Mesa as though it were a mirage.

CHAPTER 24
THE HOLTVILLE INTERLUDE

Two days later after an early start and a long drive, with the sun rising in their faces and ultimately moving down their backs, they made camp for the night at a common ground where most people who lived far west of Holtville stopped after the first day.

It was the time of the year of strong grass. The time of year Indians called "making fat." The team did not have to hop far for all the graze they needed, and although this campground, like many others close to creeks, had everything except firewood, they were comfortable because Bart had tossed a couple of armloads of that into the wagon before leaving home.

Jim was making such an elaborate effort to appear calm, as though he visited towns every month, that Bart and Nan winked at one another. But in fact they had been wrong in assuming he had never been in a large town before. Because neither of them knew much about reservations, they were unaware that every Indian reservation had at least one sizable town on its fringes. If there had not been one before the reservations had been established, there was one shortly. Reservations brought a lot of money to an area, not just with army payrolls but also through stockmen who furnished beef. The town adjacent to the reservation Jim had lived on was larger than Holtville.

But Jim's parents had gone there only very reluctantly. Although they'd never had much money, they usually had trading goods; still, that was not the reason they had rarely gone there. In reservation towns, Indians were scorned as a necessary nuisance. It was a galling experience for Jim's parents and brothers, but he had been very young then and had been too round-eyed over the size of the place and the displays of merchandise in store windows to notice much else.

Finally, about noon of the second day, with Holtville in sight, Jim told Nan and Bart of that other town. They listened without commenting but at least for Nan one source of anxiety was put to rest.

They approached from the southwest in order to enter Holtville down at the public corrals. There, Nan waited while Jim and her husband cared for the team and parked the old wagon. Holtville was a thriving community. This was particularly noticeable during the earlier hours of the day. There was considerable roadway traffic and freight outfits, huge and weathered, drawn by strings of mules or horses. There were shoppers on both side of the road and horsemen, singly or in groups, weaving in and out of the wagon and buggy traffic.

A number of ranch wagons were strung out near the general store. Nan noticed one wagon she knew from childhood. It was old but well-maintained and had her father's brand burned into both sides below the spring-seat.

They were making a diagonal crossing when a large, dark man sang out Bart's name. He was standing in overhang shade, grinning. Nan said, "Deputy Jeff Morris" to Jim, and smiled as they came up onto the duckboards beside him. Bart introduced Jim. The massively large man shoved out a hand the size of a dinner plate. "Heard about you," he told the youth. "Just this morning Charley Lord was tellin' me about what happened to your eyes. You're very lucky."

Morris raised smiling eyes to Bart. "You'll likely run into Charley and Cuff. They got in last night. Last I saw, they'd finished loadin' the wagon and went up to the pool hall."

Nan had a question. "Did you talk to Alex after he and Abel and Foster came back from making wood?"

The big man nodded. "Yep, sure did." His eyes dropped to Jim again. "He told me about you keepin' a log from smashin' em up yonder."

Nan's head was slightly to one side as she said, "Did he mention Alex's horses?"

The deputy shifted his stance. "Yes'm." He seemed reluctant to pursue this subject. "Just that your pa's riders went with Bart after some — ."

"No," she interrupted swiftly. "Did he mention anything happening to the horses while they were up at Wild Horse Mesa?"

Deputy Morris looked blankly at her and shook his head. Then he said, "Did something happen up there?"

She smiled sweetly. "Nothing important. The horses got loose is all."

As they were aiming for the large general store, Jim made a remark that indicated Nan's swift change of subject had not escaped his notice. He said, "Later, maybe he could tell us where my brothers are buried."

At the general store they both were greeted by people they had known a long time, and when Jim was introduced around no one actually seemed surprised. Bart wryly smiled to himself. Moccasin telegraph worked very fast among whiteskins, too.

Jim tried on new clothing with the obedience of any sixteen-year-old who understood the necessity of pleasing those who were buying it for him. He actually had an Indian's indifference to attire, requiring only that it prevent him from freezing in winter and roasting in summer. But the boots had him breathless. He'd owned very few new things in his life and never new boots, nor in fact had he ever imagined he would own a pair someone else had not worn first.

The old man wearing the candy-striped shirt and rimless glasses who waited on them looked up with twinkling eyes. "Walk across toward the stove," he said, "an' walk back. We got to be plumb sure they ain't too tight. Too loose don't mean much. Extra socks'll take care of that."

The old man, Nan, and Bart watched Jim cross the room and start back. A freckled face youth, slightly taller than Jim and quite a bit heavier who had been standing with his mother at the dry goods counter, watched. As Jim started back he curled his lip and said, "Hey, warwhoop, you got splayed feet. Them boots wasn't made for In'ians."

Jim stopped, turned, and looked steadily at the larger, freckled boy. Bart was motionless,

Nan clasped both hands across her stomach, and the old man in the candy-striped shirt came around from behind them with his mouth clamped hard like a bear trap. He got between the boys and shook a bony finger in the face of the freckled youth. "Lem, you had no call to say that."

The large, massive woman standing beside the freckled youth reddened. "Amos, you aren't nothing but a clerk here. You better remember how to treat customers, or I'll have a talk with Mr. Jenkins and you'll be out of a job."

The old man straightened up. Bart could see him waver and crossed to Jim, smiled and said, "Come on, son, walk. Are they tight?"

The interlude passed, but there had been a number of customers in the store who had witnessed it. As soon as Jim walked back toward the boot counter, people became busy again, mostly with their backs to the room.

The old man did not smile as he knelt to feel Jim's feet inside the boots and to gruffly ask if they pinched. They didn't, so he struggled up to his feet, pale eyes behind the rimless glasses still angry. Then he smiled. "Your name is Jim? Now then, Jim, don't pay no mind to that boy. He's got bad manners."

Nan asked who the large woman was. The old man glanced across the room and lowered his voice as he replied. "Miz Stuart. That's her son, Lem. Biggest bully around town, that boy."

Nan's brows rose slightly. "Stuart? Is she the wife of the banker?"

The old man's gaze came back. "Yes'm."

Bart paid for their purchases, handed the old man his list for supplies, said they'd be along with the rig in the afternoon, and led the way out to the roadway. He blew out a big breath and looked at his wife. Between them Jim was looking at the new boots. He seemed to have forgotten the incident, but Bart knew how good Jim was at hiding his feelings.

Someone called from up the road upon the opposite side. Abel Morrison was standing in the door of his harness shop wearing an old stained apron. He was grinning from ear to ear.

They walked over there. Abel took them inside, then stopped and stared at the new boots. As he slowly raised his face he said, "Darn. I was figuring on buyin' you a pair. I would have, only I hadn't no idea what size you'd need." He cuffed Jim roughly on the shoulder and jerked his head. "Come around behind the counter. I want to show you something."

He had been working on a new saddle with a twelve-inch seat, too small for a man. The skirts were semi-round and fully hand-carved. It was a beautiful piece of craftsmanship, and Abel was proud of it. He gestured. "Climb up and set init, Jim."

It fit, Jim admired it almost with awe, and Bart asked who Abel was making it for. The older man wiped both hands on the old soiled apron as he replied. "For Jake Stuart's boy, Lem." The silence this announcement evoked and the blank looks made Morrison stop wiping his hands. "Something wrong?"

Nan told him of the interlude at the emporium, and Abel did not look surprised; he looked disgusted. "Couldn't wait, eh? New kid so he had to get in his licks. Well, it's a nice saddle, anyway, don't you think?"

They all agreed that it was a beautiful saddle. Abel was uncomfortable. "You'd ought to go over to Alex's gun shop an' let him show you his horses. They look as good as new. He'd sure be pleased to see you folks."

He even went with them, leaving his shop open and unattended. Alex had just finished bluing someone's six-gun and had blue hands but he shook with Bart and Jim anyway because the stain did not come off. He took them out back and across the alley where he had a large shed and an even larger old corral. His big bay horses were drowsing in shed-shade over there. They knew Alex's voice, so their ears were up when he came around the shed. He stopped and shook his head. "Biggest pair of beggers this side of the Missouri River. Look at 'em, they got on their pitiful expressions. That's to make me feel bad and pitch them more feed." He turned toward Bart. "How do they look?"

They looked fine. Bart could find no sign on either horse to indicate they had been through a very bad time with the horse thieves.

Alex fixed Jim with his one eye. "Now don't get no notions, boy."

Jim smiled because he understood that he was being teased. "Do you like my boots?" he asked.

Alex made an exaggerated motion of stepping back and bending to look down. He pursed his lips and wagged his head. "When I was your age, I'd have give everything I owned for a pair of boots like them." He straightened up. "Abel and I was talkin a while back. . . . Well, it don't matter."

Abel winked. "We'll have to come up with somethin' else."

Someone hooted from across the alley. Charley Lord and Cuff were over there. Alex led the way, and as they were walking he brushed Jim's shoulder, lowered his voice, and said, "We heard from Dr. Mailer what happened up yonder. Son, now you listen to me," he touched the white patch over his eyeless socket. "Don't never take no chances with your sight. No matter what. The Lord looked after you this time, but don't count on Him being handy every time."

Charley smelled slightly of whiskey as they all trooped back to the front of the shop with its racks of guns, pistols hanging from wooden pegs, and its smell of oil. Cuff did exactly as Alex had done: he looked at the new boots, widened his eyes, and seemed to be holding his breath in shock.

Jim laughed at him.

From out in the roadway a boy's taunting call came clearly. "Hey, warwhoop. You forgot to braid your hair."

For a moment there was not a sound as the people inside turned to find the source of that shout. Abel growled under his breath. "Jake Stuart's kid." He told Charley, Cuff, and Alex what had happened over at the general store.

But it wasn't just the beefy freckled face boy; there were three other boys with him, grinning but silent. Lem Stuart was standing in the roadway with his legs wide, hands on his hips. He had very pale blue eyes and a loose, heavy mouth.

From inside the gun shop it was not possible to see much, but the shouts had caught the attention of a number of people up and down the roadway. They turned to watch as Lem Stuart yelled again. "Is that lady your ma? How come you're darker'n she is?"

Alex started for the doorway. He had the quickest temper of anyone in the shop. But he did not quite reach the opening before Charley Lord shouldered past.

The boys in the roadway lost their grins instantly. Charley was a large, rough-looking man even without his shell belt and holstered Colt. He stood upon the edge of the plank-walk to say something when Jim passed him so rapidly he could not even raise a hand in time to grab him.

Bart was directly behind Jim, but Charley threw up a large arm and growled at Bart. "Leave him be."

Nan had both hands to her mouth as Jim, thin but tall, wiry and unthinking, plowed into the large, freckled boy, fists beating the air like windmill paddles.

Lem Stuart did not give any ground even though he was hit several times, but he shifted slightly, turning his side to the flailing fists until the surprise had passed, then he came back around, face red, eyes slitted, waited until Jim rushed him again, and lashed out hard with his right fist, then with his left.

Jim was stopped in mid-stride. His mouth

opened and his eyes widened. Nan moaned and Bart ground his teeth. The Stuart boy was large and heavy. Someday he would be a man of impressive size. Right now he had successfully used his advantages to either beat or bully most of the other boys in Holtville. The ones who might have fought back had been told not to by parents who claimed that they did not believe in fist-fighting to cover up their dread of what might happen if one of their boys whipped the banker's son. Jake Stuart had loans out all over town. He was a power in Holtville country.

Jim shuffled back from the heavy hands of the freckled boy, and Alex, who was beside himself, yelled at him. "Move. Move left an' right. Jim, don't stand still."

Jim moved, but the larger boy was after him. His friends who had retreated to the far plankwalk, called shrill encouragement. Lem did not move fast, he was too heavy to move rapidly, but he could evidently hit very hard.

He staggered Jim with a blow over the heart, and that was almost too much for Cuff, who yelled, "Jim — back away, left an' right an' get around him."

Jim retreated. The boys on the far sidewalk hooted at him in derision. Nan grasped her husband's arm. "Stop it. He could be hit in the eyes. Bart . . ."

Charley, Abel, and Alex yelled. Jim had finally started weaving from left to right. Cuff said, "By gawd, he learns fast." Then he raised his voice. "That's right, Jim, keep it up, move and hit an' move."

The boys across the road were silent. There were spectators lining both sides of the roadway. They were not making a sound either, but up the road someone emerging from the brick bank building stopped to briefly watch, then ran back inside.

Jim was finally marking his opponent's face, but he did not seem to have the ability to stop him. Still, he made the Stuart boy keep away instead of boring in like a bull as he had been doing.

Nan had an iron grip on Bart's arm, but she no longer implored him to intervene. Jim crouched now, kept his body swaying, his black eyes narrowed to slits as he fought. He was not angry, which made it possible for him to calculate the Stuart boy's movements, and shortly before the fight ended, Lem Stuart, who had been struck three times in the mouth, withdrew in a flat-footed walk, let his arms drop, and panted for breath. His mouth was swelling, his shirtfront was bloody, his face was as red as a beet, and sweat dripped from his chin.

Alex called again, his voice lower this time.

"You got him, Jim. He's punky soft. Now just stab an' keep stabbin'."

But it was finished. Two large, portly men came running down the roadway from the direction of the bank. Behind them was that portly woman who had been in the emporium, but they had out-distanced her handily. The larger of the two men, wearing a vest with a massive gold chain across the lower part of it, had a coarse-featured, round fat face. It was normally pale, but right now it was pink as he bawled at the boys. He got between them, and Jim moved well away as the big man looked at his son, at the blood, the smashed swelling mouth, the baffled look in his son's eyes, and turned in a fury. "Gawd-damn you," he yelled at Jim, and started forward with balled fists. But that was not only an oversight; it was a very bad mistake.

Bart moved swiftly in behind the banker, who was raising a club-like fist, caught the back of the big man's vest, and whirled him around. They were less than eighteen inches apart, and the big man still holding his fist in the air, when Bart said, "You touch that boy, Mr. Stuart, and I'll skin you alive. Put your arm down."

The banker did not begin to lower his arm until he saw Alex, Abel, Cuff, and Charley walking toward him in the middle of the roadway, spreading out as they advanced. None of them was smiling. He lowered his arm as he said. "Is that damned In'ian kid with you, Templeton?"

Bart answered softly. "Yeah, he's with me, Mr. Stuart. You want to know who started that fight?"

Charley Lord, thumbs hooked in his shell belt, spoke up. "That damned fat bullyin' kid of yours started it, Mr. Stuart. I'm goin' to give you some advice. You better break the kid of yours to lead, because in another couple of years he's goin' to be old enough to get himself shot when he tries bullyin' someone."

Jake Stuart looked fiercely at them. "I'll remember you. Every damned one of you."

Nan spoke from the sidewalk. "And my father, Mr. Stuart. Remember him too, because on our way home I'm going to stop by and tell him exactly what happened here and what you said about remembering people." Nan did not smile, but she could have. Jake Stuart's face got pale as he stared at her. She and Jake Stuart knew who the largest depositor and shareholder was in the bank Stuart managed.

He turned slowly, still slightly out of breath, and regarded his son, who still looked dazed, probably less from being outfought than because he'd never seen his own blood on his shirtfront before. Stuart said, "Get home. You and your ma get home. . . . Lem, someday it was bound to come to this. Now you get home and I'll be along directly. *Get!*"

CHAPTER 25
DRIVING WEST

The opportunity for Jim to visit the graves of his brothers was overlooked in the excitement following the brawl in the middle of the roadway. Shortly before the Templetons left Holtville with their supplies, accompanied by Cuff and Charley Lord with the laden Holbrook rig, the men had pumped Jim's arm and cuffed him across the shoulders inside the harness shop, pleased as they could be over the results of the fight. Nan remained in the background, watching. Her expression was equal parts bleak satisfaction at the way the fight had ended, and womanly irritation over the hooting and laughing and back-slapping of her husband and the other men.

They were a mile out with the Holbrook wagon up ahead a hundred or so yards when Bart put a sidelong glance upon Jim Moore. That was what he had been convinced the lad was going to have to learn: how to settle with the bullies who would over the years sneer at his redskin background. He had thought he might have the time when they were up on Wild Horse Mesa to teach Jim what he had himself learned from experience about that sort of thing. Now, as he eyed the lad askance, he was not certain that Jim needed a whole lot of instruction. As Alex had said, the boy learned fast.

It was Nan who finally put a hand on Jim's arm and smiled as she said, "My father has always said it's best to avoid a fight if you can, and if you can't, to bore in and never look back until you've won."

Jim's hands were sore, his ribs ached, and his mind was full of the details of that encounter back in town, so he said nothing for a long while, in fact, not until the sun was directly above and they halted to water the horses in willow shade beside the creek. Then while he was helping Bart, Jim said, "When I was growin' up on the reservation, there was always someone who wanted to fight."

Bart listened and looked around for Nan. She was over where the Holbrook men were also watering their team. He said, "I figured you'd got into tangles before. You did right well. Thing is, with those big ones that can't get untracked as fast as you can, you got to keep moving from side to side. That ties 'em up because they can't shift as fast as you can. Keep 'em always off-balance, then you can whittle on 'em like you was cutting down a tree. You did good, son."

The lad held up two swollen hands. Jim laughed and pointed to the cold water. "Soak 'em. It'll help, but they'll hurt for a day or two, until the puffiness goes down."

Nan returned as the Holbrook riders re-bridled their horses, climbed up to kick off the binders, and went plowing across the creek. She did not mention the fight although that had been what had been discussed. She watched her men slip in the bits, haul back the headstalls, and come back where she was waiting.

As Bart whistled up his horses, Nan said, "They're proud of you, Jim," and that all she said about the fight for a long time.

The two outfits made a common night camp, and because the subject of the brawl had been pretty well exhausted — and also because of the look Nan put on her father's men when the topic came up — they searched for other things to discuss. Jim gave the camp-fire talk its best impetus when he mentioned Wild Horse Mesa and the possibility of catching mustangs up here.

That was always a worthwhile subject because eight of every ten rangemen had tried mustanging at one time or another. Charley reminisced. When he had finished, Cuff began. Of the two men Cuff had clearly done the most. He held his small audience spellbound relating experiences he'd had south of the border, trapping what the people down there called *mesteños*.

Bart Templeton, who had mustanged more than most rangemen, recognized in Cuff his equal. As the fire died those two were down to discussing techniques. By bedtime, although Charley and Nan were tired and Jim probably should have been except that he hung on every word Bart and Cuff said, the choice came down to hunting for more firewood or turning in. They turned in.

The following day was as beautiful as most of its predecessors had been, but by the time they reached the Holbrook yard there was enough heat to convince any doubters that springtime was gone and summer had arrived.

Nan and her father walked a little apart as the wagon Charley had tooled from town was backed to the side door of the cook shack to be unloaded.

Bart freed his team, but left their harness on as he and Jim led them out back to the stone trough. After they were tanked up, they took them back inside the barn and left them in separate stalls, still wearing their harness.

John Holbrook was waiting out near the hitch rack. When Jim emerged accompanied by Bart, the old cowman squinted at him and smiled. "There's always at least one like the Stuart boy, Jim. As old as I am, every now an' then I run into one even yet. You did exactly right. And I'll tell you something: if that boy ever bullies you again, I'll be almighty surprised. Next time I'm in town, I'll discuss a few things with his pa. Now, I'm not protecting you. You got to fight your own battles; no one can do it for you. But in this case, it's different. That boy made a remark about my daughter, and neither you nor I set back and listen to someone do that about our ladies, do we?"

Jim shook his head.

John Holbrook took them to the main house for a meal. Nan had already gone up there to start preparing it. When she looked out into the parlor and saw the three men of her life enter, she smiled.

During the meal, Jim brought up wild horses again, and when he had finished and had gone back down to the barn, Nan quietly mentioned what had disturbed her before — Jim going back up there so soon after his nightmare the time the storm had arrived.

She was talked down by both her husband and her father. She did not mention it again.

By mid-afternoon the Templetons were ready to roll again, this time over the few miles separating the big cow outfit from the smaller horse ranch. Her father, as he always seemed to do, stood alone in the yard for a long while watching them travel west. Charley Lord sauntered over, squinted against the westering sun in the direction of the rig, and said, "You should have been there."

Holbrook nodded without speaking, watching the distant wagon.

"Nan was sort of betwixt an' between. When Jim was gettin' hammered on, she wanted Bart to stop it. When he commenced catchin' on how things was done and began pepperin' that big fat kid, she did not say another word about stoppin' it."

Holbrook turned finally. "That's the way they are, Charley. If you ever get married, you'd ought to learn to look at their expressions before you do somethin' because nine times out of ten, that look'll tell you whether they're goin' to get a big smile of approval an' maybe a kiss, or get snatched bald-headed when they get you alone. . . . It keeps a man busy, I can tell you."

Charley turned his squinted gaze to his employer. "Now then, I know that is good advice, but the day I get married it's goin' to rain snowballs in hell. . . . They're goin up to the mesa after mustangs."

Holbrook already knew that. "Yeah. Nan

thinks it's too soon to take the lad up there."

Charley wagged his head. "Naw. He's tough an' he's resourceful. As long as he's with Nan and Bart, he most likely won't hardly even remember."

Holbrook thought his rangeboss had made a very good argument in favor of the boy riding to the mesa with his folks. He looked up at the taller man. "Too late for you'n Cuff to ride out an' find the other men. I'll go up to the house and fetch a bottle down to the bunkhouse and we can set and swap lies for a spell. Tell me something, Charley. Can he hit hard?"

Charley laughed and shook his head. "No. But he sure as hell can hit often. He's as fast as a strikin' snake."

"I'll go get the bottle."

The rangeboss looked again out where the buggy was no longer visible in slanting sunlight, smiled to himself, and went toward the barn to find Cuff.